After Dinner Conversation Themes
Examining The Past Edition
Philosophy | Ethics Short Story Fiction

After Dinner Conversation *Themes* – Examining the Past

This magazine publishes fictional stories that explore ethical and philosophical questions in an informal manner. The purpose of these stories is to generate thoughtful discussion in an open and easily accessible manner.

Names, characters, businesses, organizations, places, events, and incidents are either the product of the author's imagination or are used fictitiously. Any resemblance to actual persons, living or dead, events, or locales is entirely coincidental. The magazine is published monthly in print and electronic format.

ISBN 979-8-9896194-9-8 (Print)
ISBN 979-8-2248450-8-8 (Digital)
Library of Congress Control Number: 2023952698

https://www.afterdinnerconversation.com

After Dinner Conversation believes humanity is improved by ethics and morals grounded in philosophical truth and that philosophical truth is discovered through intentional reflection and respectful debate. In order to facilitate that process, we have created a growing series of short stories across genres, a monthly magazine, and two podcasts. These accessible examples of abstract ethical and philosophical ideas are intended to draw out deeper discussions with friends, family, and students.

Table Of Contents

* * *

From the Edition Editor

A life's journey is a marvelous thing–bookended by confusion and disorientation–yet between those awesome extremities there are abundant opportunities for clarity and comprehension.

We all carry memories that have been calloused over by time and forgetfulness. Each holds truths about who we were and how we lived our life. And, as much as we might want to drop them off at some memory storage facility, they persist as long as we do. The human question is, "what do we do with them while life is still in us".

The ability to reflect on the roads we have traveled, the people we have met along the way–the joys and sorrows–the times we got it right and those when we got it wrong–is one that makes us human in a way that can enrich our lives and hand us gifts that we can regift to others.

Sometimes, years afterwards, a dim light may begin to glow. When that glow grows into a spotlight, we may see things differently. And, if we are open-hearted, we may come to a new understanding of ourselves and others.

Sometimes those flashes of new insight are difficult to accept. They may show our actions in a harsh light. With others, we may be forced to confront a misunderstanding that has led us astray. A decision in youth may bring regret and, much later, lead us to find ways to seek redemption. Or sometimes events simply bring us yet again face-to-face with a traumatic event and allow us to see it in a new light.

In the end, we are left with the fleeting ability to reflect on our journey and, in calmer and more reflective moments, harvest new understandings that may make us better people in the future. The stories in this anthology are about those times and new understandings. Each on a different road. Some reach a new understanding, while others turn away. Each protagonist faced that most human question. How they found their answers may help you along in your journey.

Earl R. Smith II, PhD – Edition Editor

The Man Who Killed the Dog

Robert Collings

* * *

Trigger Warning: This story contains violence against a dog. In short, it's a tough read.

* * *

When I was a child, I often worried over my busy thoughts, and how those thoughts could never seem to keep up with the complicated world around me. "Oh, that's no cause to worry," my grandma assured me. "Life gives a person a lot to think about." I have always found comfort in Grandma's wise words, especially when I've seen that complicated world reflected in the eyes of others.

* * *

I was going to university full-time, and in the summer months I worked wherever I could in order to ease the burden of my student loans. One year I was lucky enough to land a summer job stocking shelves at night at Lowrey's Market, a huge supermarket that was only a block away from my basement suite.

Jimmy Boone was one of the guys on the night crew. These were the guys who bought loads of lotto tickets and dreamed about winning a fortune. Jimmy was a lanky, skinny character, a good six feet tall, with lots of blond hair and a freewheeling attitude that set him apart from the more solemn guys on the crew. He was a full-time employee and he'd worked nights for a few years running. This meant that he was up all night and slept during the day, but his face was always flushed and ruddy-cheeked, as if he had just stepped out of the sunshine. He looked like a landlocked surfer dude. I didn't have much in common with Jimmy, but once he found out I wanted to go to law school he rarely left me alone.

"I want to tell everyone I know a university guy!" he would proclaim with a big smile. I had recently read a biography about the life and times of King George IV, a notorious brandy drinker in his early years. Jimmy and I had been talking about how people liked to drink alcohol, even kings and queens in the old days. I told Jimmy about the title "Prince Regent" and how this was a designation that had been given to George IV when his father was still alive but was too out of it to do anything useful. Jimmy got a kick out of the story and he picked up on the name. Whenever he saw me arrive at work, he would always exclaim, "Here comes the Prince Regent!"

I had never had anyone refer to me by such an exalted title, and I began to think that all the worry and all the sweating over the books might not be such a bad thing after all.

Jimmy Boone was a couple of years older than me, but he reminded me of those kids in the movies who suddenly find themselves trapped inside the body of an adult and then spend the rest of the movie trying to act like a grown-up. In these silly comedies, the only ones who don't seem to be fooled are the other children. Jimmy was an impromptu kind of guy, always joking around and bursting at the seams with kid-energy. He had the agility of an acrobat. He would tell a joke and then emphasize the punchline with a series of crazy backflips down the aisle until he reached the far end of the store. "Anything for a yuck!" he would yell out as we all cracked up. "I have no shame!"

There seemed to be a darker side to Jimmy, a darker past, but I never asked him about it. His forearms were covered with tattoos before tattoos had ever become fashionable. They were crudely drawn and without color, and I knew jailhouse tattoos when I saw them even before I began defending criminals. None of the other guys on the crew ever had a bad word to say about Jimmy, and I figured he'd worked out his wild streak long before I ever came along. He was married with two preschool-age children. I never socialized with Jimmy outside the store, but at the produce manager's retirement party, I found myself sitting next to Jimmy's wife, Trudy.

She was a pretty girl, barely out of high school. We were watching Jimmy on the dance floor, whooping it up with a few of the store cashiers. We hadn't said a word to each other all night. Without any pretense of small talk, she turned to me and said in a childlike voice, "Jimmy's sensitive about his lack of education. He says you're the smartest person he's ever known, but he can still tell you things and you're a good listener. That's why he admires you."

The sincerest form of flattery is not imitation at all. It's hearing wonderful things said about you through a third person you barely know. I thought Jimmy Boone was okay, tattoos and all.

Jimmy and I were working side-by-side early one morning, and we were about halfway through our shift. We were alone in the aisle next to the produce department, and the two other members of the crew were on the other side of the store. Jimmy had been quiet that night. He hadn't told any jokes, and he hadn't done a single backflip. We were working close together, stocking the shelves and then bringing everything to the front with the labels all lined up. I was working away, lost in my own thoughts, when I turned casually to Jimmy and I noticed that he had stopped working. He was still close beside me, and he was staring at the palm of his outstretched hand. I immediately thought that he had cut his hand with his box cutter.

"Hey, is your hand okay?" I asked.

His response took me by surprise. "Do they teach psychology at that university you go to?" he asked.

"Yes," I replied. "They teach everything."

Jimmy was still staring at his hand. "Did you ever take any psychology courses?"

"I took one as an elective in first year," I said. "I wasn't into it. The professor wanted to go on and on about the central nervous system, and I tuned out."

Jimmy then lowered his hand and faced me. The familiar grin had been absent all night, and he now had a worried look. "Keep working, keep working," he said quietly. "I don't want that lead man asshole to come around and give us shit. Do psychologists help you when you have thoughts you don't want?

I'm bothered by something."

I went back to stocking the shelf and Jimmy inched a little closer to me. "You have to promise me that you'll never tell anybody in the world what I'm going to tell you."

I hesitated. "Well, if you plan to rob the store—"

"Shut up," Jimmy said. "Shut up and keep working. You're not a lawyer yet. Promise me."

"Okay, I promise."

Jimmy looked around to make sure no one was going to overhear us. "I was a crazy person when I was a kid," he said. "I had decent parents and my brother and sister were normal. I was the crazy one. There was another person inside of me and that person did things I regret doing."

I tried to empathize with him. I said, "I did some crazy things in high school, too. We had a reunion and I knew what everyone was thinking. Made me cringe."

Jimmy shook his head. "No, no, no," he said. "I did... things." There was a pause and Jimmy looked around once again to make sure we were alone. "I hung with a bad crowd, but I don't blame them. Two of the guys are dead, and one is in prison. I did a couple of stints in jail as a juvenile, no big deal. I saw the light. I straightened out. But I did things. I did things you can't take back."

Jimmy looked straight at me. I had stopped working and I was staring at him. He said, "Keep working, dammit. Somebody's gonna come around."

Once again, I started back stocking the shelf and Jimmy looked over his shoulder. "We'd steal cars, we'd do shit," he continued. "One of us, the guy now in prison, Gary, he had this old dog. The dog had this gray muzzle and it was old-old-old.

Old and sick. Gary thought his family was gonna have to put the dog to sleep, but his mother couldn't do it. She couldn't bring herself to drive it to the vet. So we thought it would be a hoot to go get the dog and kill it so his mother wouldn't have to take that drive. We all laughed about how we'd be doing his mother a favor."

Jimmy had turned his head away, but now he turned back and looked straight at me to see my reaction. I dreaded what was coming, but I kept a straight face and nodded for him to continue.

Jimmy's voice was now a whisper. "We stole a car and drove it over to his mother's place. Gary went in and got the dog and brought it out to the car. He put it in the back seat where I was sitting. The dog was ancient, I mean it was gonna have to be put to sleep any day. You could tell by just looking at it. It was this big, black dog, a Lab or something. Gary pushed the dog in beside me and then he got back behind the wheel and just roared down the street. We were drunk, we were all laughing. The dog was right beside me and it was licking my hand, like it knew what was gonna happen and it was trying to be friendly or something. Gary got to the highway and just floored it. Then he yelled back to us, 'Throw him out! Throw him out!'"

Jimmy had told me to keep working, but I was now frozen.

"I cracked open the door," he went on. "I mean, we were all just laughing so hard. The guy beside me and the guy in the front seat, we all grabbed the dog and just pushed it out onto the road. Gary drove on a bit and then did a U-turn and came back and stopped the car and we all piled out to have a look at the dog. It was lying on the side of the road. It was still breathing.

We hadn't killed it. So we shoved the dog back into the car and Gary took off to try again. The dog was right beside me. It was making squealing noises and there was blood coming from its nose, and it licked my hand again. That poor dog was licking my hand, over and over. Gary floored it and screamed out, 'Kill it again!' and we all laughed like crazy and pushed the dog out onto the road a second time. Gary turned the car around and we found the dog lying in a heap, this time right in the middle of the road. It was dead, finally. We drove around a bit more, then Gary ditched the car and we all went home like nothing happened."

Jimmy had turned away again and he would not look at me. All I could say was, "That's an awful story. It's the worst story I ever heard."

"You hate me now," Jimmy said.

"I don't hate you, Jimmy," I said quietly. "I hate what you did."

"You hate me, and I shouldn't have told you," Jimmy said.

"Have you told that story to anybody else?" I asked.

"No. Well, just that doctor the one time. The bunch of us, we never even talked about it afterward."

"What doctor is this?"

"I couldn't sleep," Jimmy whispered, still looking away. "I saw this doctor. It's a secret; Trudy doesn't know about it. He told me to read some story about a rich guy who kills animals and then feels all this guilt and goes to Heaven or something. He gave me some pills."

Jimmy was talking about a story by Flaubert, and I knew he hadn't read a thing. "Jimmy, why on this earth did you decide to tell me this?"

Jimmy lowered his head. "I gotta get it off my chest," he whispered. His voice was so low that I could barely hear him. "I gotta talk to someone else. I'm still not sleeping. Something's happening to me."

Just then, the lead man on the crew called us for lunch and my conversation with Jimmy came to an end. He didn't try to bring up the subject after the break, and we worked apart for the rest of the night.

A couple of weeks after Jimmy's early morning confession, he announced to the crew that he was quitting his job at Lowrey's and was taking a sales job with someone he'd met at his karate class. I didn't get all the details, but the job had something to do with perfumes and scents. The hook was supposed to be that brand-name perfumes have a huge markup, and this company sold the same thing for a fraction of the price. Once people used the product, they never went back to store-bought perfumes again. All you had to do was build up a large enough client base and you could just sit back and fill orders and watch the money roll in.

I wasn't surprised to hear that Jimmy's new dream job lasted about twelve days before he was on the phone to the store manager begging for his old job back. The manager liked Jimmy, as we all did, but the answer was no. Guys like Jimmy were expendable because they were never going to make it into any management level no matter how long they stuck around. They would all be buying lotto tickets forever. Jimmy was never even going to make it to lead man on the crew for an extra fifty cents an hour, which was a nothing job. Those guys were never given a second chance when they'd blown the chance they had, and Jimmy was no exception.

After he'd been turned down, I was surprised when Jimmy called and asked me to speak to the store manager to try to get him to change his mind.

"Jimmy, I'm a part-time guy on the night crew," I laughed. "He barely knows me. You think I'm just gonna walk up and speak to him and get your job back for you?"

"Well, not exactly," Jimmy replied.

"Is that the real reason you called me, to ask me this?"

"Well, not exactly," Jimmy said again.

There was a long silence. I knew why Jimmy had called, and I was waiting for him to bring up the subject.

"Do you remember the story I told you?" Jimmy asked. His voice was breaking, and I wondered how long he'd planned the phone call.

"Yes, I remember," I said.

There was a pause, and then Jimmy's voice took on a tone of desperate urgency that frightened me. "You have to believe me when I tell you," he begged. "The person who did that awful thing, the person in the car, it wasn't me. It was a person inside of me who I don't know any more. That person won't leave my body, he won't leave me alone. He killed that dog. I don't know what to do. You've got to forgive me."

"Jimmy, I forgive you," I insisted. "That's not what you need—"

"It was this other person, not me. I swear, I swear." Then Jimmy started to make these low, guttural sounds: "Oh, oh, oh..."

There's no comfort you can offer anyone in such a state. All I could muster was, "Jimmy, you've got to speak to somebody."

He was sobbing now, choking out the words. "I'm sorry,

I'm so sorry. Oh, I'd do anything to take it back..."

"Jimmy—"

"I told you I spoke to somebody," Jimmy mumbled through his tears. "I couldn't even pronounce the name of the stupid story I was supposed to read. It's no use, it's hopeless."

I attempted to reason with him. "You have to try, don't you? Give it a shot, give it the best shot you have."

"I gave it a shot. I took the pills. It's no use."

"I can't argue about this, Jimmy," I said. "I've got things to do. School starts up next week, my last night in the store is tonight. I'm going to be a busy guy. Dammit, you've got to talk to somebody."

"You're the only person in the world I can talk to," he said.

"Jimmy please—"

"No—"

"Please—"

"I'm cracking up."

With those last words, Jimmy ended the call, and I heard no more from him.

I had saved up enough money to travel the following summer. I didn't work and I wasn't in touch with anyone from the supermarket. I'd heard from somebody that Jimmy had found a job on the docks, and then lost that job. I wasn't sure about the details and I made no inquiries. Jimmy was still with his wife, as far as I knew. I didn't want to worry about Jimmy Boone. He had never called me again and I felt a great sense of relief. I had made it into law school and I had my own plans for my life.

I was still living in the same basement suite, and I was just finishing off my second year. I came out of the basement one morning to catch the bus to campus and saw Trudy Boone leaning against her car at the foot of the driveway. I had not seen her since our brief conversation at the store function. She looked hardened now and much older than her years. She was slouched against the car, furiously smoking a cigarette. When she saw me she tossed the cigarette aside and rushed up to me, blocking my path on the driveway before I could reach the sidewalk. Her voice was frantic, and there was no hint left of the young mother at the party.

"Do you remember me?" she said. "Jimmy's wife?"

"Yes," I said, "I remember you."

She reacted as if she had not heard me at all. "My name is Trudy. Do you remember meeting me?"

"Yes, yes," I repeated, more sharply now. "I remember. You're Trudy, Jimmy's wife. I know you. I've got to get to class."

Before I could move, she inched closer to me. Her eyes were puffy and red and I could see that she had been crying. "You've got to help Jimmy," she pleaded. "You've got to do something."

"Trudy, I can't help Jimmy," I said. "If he needs help, he's got to find it somewhere else. I've told him this. I know he heard me because I screamed it at him. There's nothing I can do."

"You're his best friend—" she began.

"I'm not his best friend," I interrupted. I was now being harsh with her and I felt guilty. "I haven't talked to him in ages. I haven't seen him. He shouldn't be telling you these things."

"He says you're his best friend—"

"Stop saying that, please—"

"He has no other friends," she pleaded. "He won't talk to anybody. He got fired from the docks for not showing up. He lost all his benefits; we can't afford doctors. He doesn't know who his children are, he just ignores them. When he's not going on about some stupid dog and how he's going to burn in hell, he keeps saying you're his best friend. He keeps saying he can talk to you because you understand. You have to help him, we're all going crazy!"

I felt true sympathy for this lady, but her journey to my driveway had been pointless. I said, "Trudy, you've got to understand, there's nothing I can do."

"You've got to talk to him!" she screamed. "You've got to help him!"

I moved to leave and she hurled herself at me as if to tackle me to the pavement. I backed away and she stumbled forward, but she kept her balance. In that moment I was able to hustle across the lawn and head down the sidewalk, and I did not stop moving until I reached the far end of the block. When I finally stopped and turned back to the house, I saw that she hadn't bothered to follow me. I watched her get back into her car and then head off in the opposite direction.

I never saw Trudy Boone again after that conversation, and I never spoke to her. I had no communication at all with Jimmy until many years later. What I'm going to tell you now has been patched together from a number of sources, including a junior lawyer in our office who had worked as a paramedic in the emergency radius where Trudy and Jimmy once lived.

After that scene with Trudy Boone in the driveway, Jimmy apparently found the strength to make some progress with his life. I don't know what caused this. It may have been Trudy's account of our conversation that started him thinking, I never really found out. Unlike his failed attempt to get back on the night crew at Lowrey's, Jimmy was able to land a job again on the docks and he seemed to be doing okay. He showed up for work on time and never missed a shift. He never phoned in sick, and never did a thing to ruffle the feathers of his fellow workers or the union or anyone else. By all accounts, he became a different man at home, too. He drew closer to his children and got involved in their activities. He socialized when the occasion arose, and never caused a stir. Trudy stopped worrying about him. She was thrilled that the demons that had been haunting her husband, the demons that had led her to my driveway, were now long gone. People have temporary setbacks in their lives, but people get over it. That's what this was, a temporary setback that now belonged to a distant past.

One morning, Trudy woke up and Jimmy was not in the bed next to her. Jimmy was not scheduled to work that day, and he liked to sleep late when he had the day off. On those days, she had always been the first one to get out of bed. Jimmy was not in the bedroom, and he was not in the hallway. When she came downstairs and entered the kitchen, she saw Jimmy at the sink with his back to her. He had a hammer in his right hand and he was resting the hammer on the countertop. She called his name, but he didn't respond and he didn't budge. Alarmed, she stepped cautiously up to him and it was only when she got close that she saw what he had done.

Jimmy had his left hand pressed flat against the counter with his palm up and his thumb and fingers extended. He had managed to use his free hand to pound a long spike-nail through the upright palm and then all the way into the countertop until his hand was welded onto the linoleum and wouldn't budge. He had pounded with such determination that there was less than an inch of the nail now sticking up out of the skin. The nail had barely missed the radial artery where it arches near the knuckles or he would have bled to death long before Trudy had discovered him. As it was, there was surprisingly little blood and Jimmy did not seem to be in any distress. He did not say anything when Trudy came upon the macabre scene and started screaming. She was still hysterical when help arrived, but the paramedics reported that Jimmy was placid and simply gazing out the window when they burst into the kitchen. One of them noted that he had his face pressed close to the glass with his chin tilted slightly upwards, as if he were checking out the clouds. Even when they began the grim task of holding Jimmy's arm and wrist tight to the counter while they pulled the nail out of his hand, he remained composed and silent. The extraction took a while due to the hard surface of the counter and the depth of the nail, but Jimmy didn't complain and he never resisted. All he reportedly said was, "It doesn't hurt, you know. It really doesn't hurt at all."

After a stint in emergency, they took Jimmy to the psych ward at Royal Inland where he stayed a few months. He hadn't been very vocal during his early stint in hospital, although he was apparently willing to give a brief communication when he was hungry or when he had to go to the bathroom. By the time he was transferred to the facility up in Redmond, he had stopped speaking. At times he would point or give a slight gesture to indicate what he wanted or what he was thinking, but that soon ended and he stopped communicating altogether. They brought him food and he would eat when he was hungry. If he wasn't hungry, the food would be left untouched on the tray. The staff in Redmond learned to deal with him on a strict timeline. He would get out of bed at a certain time, eat at a certain time, go to the bathroom twice a day on an exact schedule. Bath time was twice a week and he was always docile and compliant. The rest of the time he just sat in his wheelchair with his head down and his eyes focused upon the scar on the palm of his hand. He would carefully place his hand upright on the arm of the wheelchair and stare down for hours, locked into his own thoughts and unaware of his surroundings. If he did know where he was, his body and his eyes gave up no clue.

The long-term care facility in Redmond became Jimmy's permanent home. Trudy divorced him and his children grew up and drifted away. I thought about Jimmy from time to time, but I had lots of other things to think about, too, and Jimmy Boone gradually found a place in the back of my memory.

About thirty years had gone by since my conversation in the driveway with Trudy. Then, seemingly out of nowhere, I got a telephone call from one of the psychiatrists up at Redmond. He had a young-sounding voice, something that was now becoming a constant reminder of my own advancing years. After telling me who he was, the first thing this doctor wanted to know was my full name, and I naively complied. I have spent my professional lifetime warning clients not to disclose any personal information on a phone call, and there I was, spelling out my name like some nervous schoolboy on the first day of class. I'm ashamed to admit that my superstitions had got the better of me, and I thought that my immediate cooperation might somehow guarantee me a lifetime immunity from ever having to do a stint at the John J. Redmond hospital for the insane.

Once he was satisfied that he was speaking to the right

person, the young doctor got right down to business. "Do you know a man named Jimmy Boone?" he asked politely.

"Yes, I used to work with him."

"Are you the person he used to call the Prince Regent?"

"Yes, that's me."

"Well, we've been looking for you for quite a while."

"Jimmy needs a roommate, does he?"

The doctor chuckled, but it was a hollow sound. "Not quite. Mr. Boone hasn't spoken in a number of years, but some time back he handed one of the orderlies a piece of paper with the name 'Prince Regent' written on it."

"That's all? Just that name?"

"That's all. He doesn't speak and there's been no more writing. He had a wife once, but she's long gone. It took a bit of effort to figure out who you were."

"You found me," I said. "So, what do you want with me?"

"We thought it might be helpful if you came out and said hi to Jimmy."

"You want me to come up to Redmond?"

"Not to admit you," the doctor said. "Just to say hi. Maybe that'll help out, maybe not. Worth a chance, don't you think?"

"This was a lifetime ago," I said. "Is Jimmy okay, is he healthy?"

"He's okay," the doctor replied. "He just doesn't say anything."

I hesitated. "I don't know about this," I said warily.

The doctor knew what I was thinking. "Don't worry," he said. "If you want padded cells and bars on the windows, you can read something out of Dickens. Redmond's a modern place. We're proud of it, really."

The doctor had been right about the Redmond facility. From the street, the place could have been an office complex full of dentists and tech support workers. Jimmy's room was on the fifth floor. The building had one of those huge elevators that move at a crawl, and when we finally got to the top floor, I remarked to the orderly how quiet everything seemed.

"This is long-term care," the orderly said as he led me down the silent corridor. "You start out on the first floor if they think there's any hope for you. By the time you graduate to the penthouse, you don't have a heck of a lot to say." Before we entered Jimmy's room the orderly lowered his voice. "He just stares at his hand all day. It's like the hand speaks to him or something."

The orderly escorted me into the tiny room. Jimmy was in his wheelchair over in the corner. He was staring blankly at his outstretched palm, exactly the way the orderly had described him. "Visitor," the orderly announced, cheerfully. Jimmy looked up briefly at me, impassive, and then turned his attention back to his hand. I hadn't laid eyes upon Jimmy in over thirty years, but I'd heard about the nail and I was surprised to see that the scar was much smaller than I'd expected. In fact, his hand had healed to the point where you'd have to look closely to see anything out of the ordinary. Jimmy may have thought this way, too, and that was why he was so obsessed with the lingering scar. This was a mark that had faded with time, and perhaps Jimmy thought that his torment might also fade away if only the scar would vanish forever.

I was also surprised at how little Jimmy had changed over the years. Incredibly, he still had his surfer-dude complexion. His hair was thinner and he was hospital-skinny, but I would have known him anywhere. A part of me even expected him to spring up from his wheelchair and start doing his goofball cartwheels, as if the last three decades had all been part of some grand practical joke. But Jimmy just sat there, staring down, unmoved and unimpressed by my sudden presence in his life after all those years. I looked at the orderly and shrugged, uncertain what to do next.

"Maybe he wants you out of the room," I suggested.

The orderly shrugged back at me and walked out. I watched as he quietly closed the door, then I turned back to Jimmy. I watched Jimmy stare at the mark on his palm. There was no revealing sadness in his eyes, no hint of any drama, no defining look at all. I was reminded of the way the paramedics had described him in the kitchen that morning, a man with a nail through his hand who was looking blankly out the window at the weather. I said, "Jimmy, they say you don't speak, but I know you can hear me."

Jimmy nodded ever so slightly. "They say you wrote that name down," I continued in a whisper. "I know you remember me, and I know you did that for a reason."

Jimmy nodded again. I said, "Then tell me the reason, and I'll leave you alone."

Jimmy didn't speak, but he raised his hand from the arm of the wheelchair and held out his open palm in front of me. This was not a feeble motion at all, but more like a deliberate gesture that had been rehearsed. He held his hand steady for a good ten seconds and I stared straight at the small, round scar exactly as he wanted me to do. Then, Jimmy moved both hands slowly up to his temples and he began to shake his head, as if expressing confusion but unable to find the words. He was crying now but making no sound. I watched him cradle his forehead in his hands and move his head back and forth, back and forth, until I could no longer bear to be a part of all the silent despair and I had to call the orderly.

"He won't say anything," I told the orderly as soon as he came back into the room. "I think it's time for me to go."

The orderly secured Jimmy's wheelchair, and then we walked back down the long hallway to the elevator. He was curious about our exchange. He said, "The only thing the guy ever communicates is some code name on a piece of paper, and he doesn't have a word to say to you."

"That's right," I said. "Not a word."

"All that time and nothing to say," the orderly observed.

"He didn't have to say anything," I responded.

"He expects us to read his thoughts," the orderly said. "A lot of them do that."

I remembered my grandma's words of wisdom. "Thinking about things isn't so bad," I said. "Life gives a person a lot to think about."

* * *

This story first appeared in the After Dinner Conversation—May 2022 issue.

Discussion Questions

1. Do you think Jimmy deserves to be able to move on from the horrible thing he helped do, or is he getting the lifetime of punishment he deserves? Are there acts so terrible that a person never should be allowed to move on from it?
2. Why do you think Jimmy was never able to come to terms with his horrible action and move forward with his life?
3. If you were the narrator in this story, would you have done more to help Jimmy recover? What would you have advised Jimmy to do?
4. Jimmy feels true regret and is tortured daily, while a truly horrible person would feel no regret and live a blissful remainder of his life. How do you reconcile the moral justice in these different outcomes?
5. The typical advice for Jimmy is that he needs to "forgive himself" for his past mistake. How do you convince someone to do that? How do you convince yourself?

* * *

The Free Will Of Professor Sturmhauser

Rosalind Goldsmith

* * *

Professor Sturmhauser stands in front of his students, looking focused and casually in command—it's a good disguise. Now he's pacing back and forth, tossing a pen in the air and saying this: "If you take the measure of your will, what do you think you'll find? You won't find a damn thing because there is no such thing as *will*. It's nothing but a word. A word we invented that points to a well-fed assumption that we have some control and some choice in our lives." He shrugs. "It's not true. We want it to be true, but it's not. It's only after we do something that 'choice' comes into play, and then, of course, it's not choice; it's post-factum rationalization. And when we invoke the notion of free will—we're doing so merely to flatter ourselves and our miserable existence." There are no questions this afternoon, and he gathers up his notes and computer and drives home.

He collapses onto his sofa, exhausted. He doesn't believe

everything he says—he's too tenured, too jaded for that—but he believes a hell of a lot of it, and he passionately believes this: free will is a pink unicorn with bells on its hooves, and choice is a Nemean lion with fairy wings and a bright red nose.

His students—some would call them disciples—take up the cause and discuss this idea amongst themselves—this brutish, unkind, and reductive idea that their choices have really been made for them before they make them—on so many different levels, they say, it would be impossible to deconstruct the framework of the idea. Besides, there's a neurological truth to it. What it boils down to is: they are not who they think they are. They are nothing but little programmed automatons, obeying the dictates of a preternatural biological imperative: Go on! Live! Go on—live in this way, live in that way. In these circumstances, do this so you can live, and in those circumstances, do that so you can continue to live; and then do this so your offspring will live on after you, and in this way do this, and in that way do that so you can go on. You can live. Go on, then, live! Go on and live!

God! It is depressing. And their professor is a depressing soul, seeing things in this way, and there isn't a speck of joy in him and not a flicker of humor. Every lecture is bleak and punishing. It takes them down every time. In their discussions, some of them decide not to hand in their term papers but to hand in a sheaf of blank pages with a small note attached: *I did not choose not to write this paper.* Only the fear of failing the course prevents them from doing so. The professor does not take kindly to whimsy.

Some of his students wonder about his private life. Does their professor, who lives alone—they know that much—does he find any sense of meaning or purpose or joy in his life? How could he? If he lives as he wishes to live—purely according to his beliefs—as he's told them he does, then how can purpose or meaning or joy exist when there is no choice?

They imagine this: a dry and bitter and task-bound life. A teak desk, walls lined with bookshelves filled with heavy tomes—a few of them his own, a reading lamp with a gooseneck, their professor seated at his desk until two in the morning marking their papers, then reading Hume, then marking their papers, then reading Hobbes, then marking their papers, then reading Schopenhauer. Then returning to mark their papers and scrawl upon them his sharp, unforgiving comments:

"Why on earth would you ever attempt to prove this thesis?"

"At what point in grade eight were you expelled from grammar class?"

"What language are you intending to use here?"

And they imagine him going out at the same time every morning for a long walk, just like Kant.

What they never imagine is this: their esteemed professor lying whey-faced, sap-bodied, and slack-jawed on his couch, staring up at the dreary tapioca ceiling for hour upon hour, then going to the refrigerator and taking out a three-pound tub of Oreo-chip ice cream from the freezer and eating the whole tub in one sitting. With a teaspoon. Then vaguely focusing his vanilla-smeared eyes on an eighty-five-inch flat screen in front of him which displays YouTube videos of baby owls, foul-mouthed cockatoos, goats, Shetland ponies wearing sweatshirts, and a miniature donkey that clatters around someone's living room and jumps up onto a sofa.

They can't possibly imagine the amount of vodka he consumes from one evening to the next, nor the number of Percodan and Ativan he swallows, nor the 1970s made-for-TV movies he watches and enjoys to an ecstatic degree. All of this, of course, entirely without any contribution from that pink unicorn with bells, namely his *will*. He neither chose to live like this, nor did he not choose to live like this. It simply evolved to be so, every neurologically predetermined microaction leading to the next, and he is simply a non-willing participant of this evolution.

Whether this is actually the case or not, whether his will has been involved in this evolution or not, and whether his way of life has come to be because of his will, in spite of it, or entirely without it (as he would claim), some sort of collapse is imminent. He suspects it himself. He falls behind in his marking; his comments become more and more acidic and at the same time vague and disconnected; his written notes take on the characteristics of deranged spiders; he begins to arrive late for his lectures, sometimes absent his notes, and sometimes absent any idea of what he's supposed to be talking about.

Just last week, he began a lecture on Nietzsche, rambled on about Socrates and how he and Jesus of Nazareth should have been imprisoned in the same cell and beaten to a pulp, then added such a thing would be redundant. This lecture ended with a paean—to birds—especially certain kinds of birds, such as cockatoos and owls. By the end of this lecture, some of his students were baffled. Others, giving him the too-generous benefit of their plunging doubt, said that owls were a symbol of wisdom, and cockatoos were a symbol of—but they couldn't imagine what cockatoos might symbolize, and so were left to wait for their professor's view on this in his next lecture. They would certainly ask.

His students appear in the hall on Thursday afternoon for this lecture, prepared to ask him many questions. But their professor is absent. A new and young TA is standing at the lectern, replacing the professor with the accuracy of a well-rehearsed understudy. Even the gestures are similar. Not a word as to what has happened to their esteemed Professor Sturmhauser. Not one word.

His students imagine all kinds of scenarios, including hospitalization in a mental health institution, where he sits on the edge of a metal bed, head in hands in Dostoevskian despair, and where he sits at a small metal desk and writes of this despair with a fountain pen. Or they imagine he has fled to a cabin in the Waldenesque woods to find peace and sits at a small wooden desk with holes in it and writes by candlelight as he listens to the hooting of owls.

The thing they cannot imagine is the truth: that the night following his last lecture, he is found at two in the morning kneeling in a rowboat on Lake Ontario, stark naked, head lolling over the side of the boat, hands in the water, and drifting out to the middle of the lake toward Niagara Falls. He is spotted by a concerned citizen walking his hyperactive whippet in the middle of the night, who reports the sighting to the police. The police are told that it appears to be a very dangerous situation—the man seems about to haul something out of the water or to pitch himself into it—and he is also screaming—something about Zinedine Zidane. Or that's what it sounds like. The police arrive quickly, fish him out of the lake, wrap him in a blanket, and take him to a safe place.

His students would no doubt be shocked and disheartened to know that their esteemed professor has collapsed utterly. And if they knew the story of how he collapsed, they might wonder if he has fallen victim to the consequences of his own ideas—if there could be such a thing as free will, after all, and if the abandonment of it in one's personal life might not be such a good idea. And as a result of all this wondering, they might eventually renounce their beloved professor and start believing in someone else, like Elon Musk, and then drop the Philosophy 101 course, saying it was all a mistake anyway; they've always wanted to pursue a career in marketing. They might even ridicule their professor and chuckle at his demise—though if you're Professor Sturmhauser sitting in the back of a police car, shivering in a gray blanket that smells of diesel oil, there is nothing funny about it. Nothing funny at all.

But his students know none of this. They continue to wonder what has happened to him and sometimes discuss the possibilities—which always have the ring of Baudelaire, Rimbaud, or Keats—but they do not lose faith in him or his ideas.

They never find out that he is now in Fairview Rehabilitation Centre and is forbidden all alcohol and drugs and all sharp instruments. Every morning, afternoon, and evening he eats at a small table in the communal dining room. As he waits for his meal, he sits and stares at the cardboard menu with bitten edges which announces, in a haphazard and—he believes—personally insulting mix of cursive and printed letters: pork and beans on Wednesdays, chicken and rice on Thursdays, and an unnamable kind of fish on Fridays. It's always the same. There is never any variation.

At certain moments, when his mind is coherent enough to see the contradiction, he wonders why he has been given a menu at all. Then he smiles at the aptness of the metaphor. And when his mind is really sharp, he circles the spelling mistakes with his finger—apple pie a la node, pork and beens, surgeon with fried poetatoes. Surgeon?— ah, *sturgeon*, Friday's offering, which is so obviously not sturgeon but fried fish sticks containing cat food.

If he eats in his room, which he is occasionally allowed to do, he is given plastic bowls and rubber utensils to eat with. Every night a practical nurse or support worker visits his room on the hour and on the half to make sure that he is asleep, has not consumed any smuggled substances, and has not taken the bolted bars off the windows and thrown himself out. When he goes for a slow and stumbling walk in the garden after breakfast, his room is meticulously searched for any offending objects or comestibles.

During his first few weeks, he calls this institution "the Horror" and sometimes, "the Horror, the Horror, the Horror." He is stripped of all his beloved habits—Ativan, vodka, late-night videos, Oreo-chip ice cream, 3:00-a.m. bedtime—and he suffers daily the pain of withdrawal—his head spins, his stomach lurches, his arms and legs are constantly twitching—and when he tries to walk, his knees sometimes lock, and he kicks out and plunges to the floor. His meds don't help at all. He can't sleep and sometimes is not sure if he is awake or if he is hallucinating this hell.

His twenty-four-year-old daughter, Bea, who checked him in here, acknowledges his suffering but says the detox is necessary and that this respite from the stress of teaching is the best thing for him right now. She tells him he must endure it for at least six months until he is clean and can return to the university to take up his tasks once again. And if he does especially well, it might only be four months. She asks him if he agrees with her plan. "Blub blub," he says and then blows raspberries at her—not because he has lost his mind, but because—in this moment—he sees clearly the implication of this situation and responds to it in what he believes is an appropriate manner.

Bea visits him every Saturday and brings him British mystery novels to read, such as *Twilight in Twickenham* and *The Search for the Blue Danube Diamond*. He throws them out without reading them and sits on the edge of his bed, his head in his hands—much as his students have imagined him—wondering why, oh, why his own daughter—his own flesh and blood—would bring him these books. He adores her—has always adored her—calls her his *Beatrice Eterna*, but she does not understand him. And at times, she is an intolerable nuisance. The worst of it is she has a tendency to behave exactly like his ex-wife—she reads the same kind of books and takes the same esoteric, la-la vitamins: vitamin K, vitamin D3—or is it 4—and something called *Lactobasilisk Acid Adulterous*. Or something. When she comes to visit, he tells her he is utterly miserable and does not see the point in going on. She encourages him to be patient; his health will improve.

And after six weeks or so, the physical pain, dizziness, and nausea do begin to diminish. He considers the possibility that this place is not quite the ninth circle of hell. In fact, were it not for his daughter's hectoring visits, he realizes that he might, after a time, even come to experience something like contentment here. After all, there is nothing he need do, and nothing to worry about. There is not even anything to *choose* from. Every activity is chosen for him, every object he comes into contact with is predetermined down to the last fish stick and drop of toothpaste, and in this way, he can live as he wishes, according to his own ideas of a life of no will—without even having to think about it.

And he even wonders if his current circumstances might perhaps be better than they were before his collapse, inasmuch as the imposed order here does not allow him to fall prey to his own habits—which he admits is probably a good thing.

And so, Professor Sturmhauser should be—if not content—at least somewhat hopeful. He's living in harmony with his beliefs, he's purging himself of his bad habits, and he still has his job and his devoted students to return to. But he is not hopeful. Something—some tiny splinter is scraping its way into his mind. What is it, though? What? When he goes to bed, he tries to reason what the thing is, but he can't put his finger on it.

He starts here: he knows it's correct—no, *necessary*—to live in accordance with one's principles and that not to do so would create the kind of lived contradiction that leads to out-and-out hypocrisy and moral defeat. And so, he has tried to live his life in exact accordance with his ideas, in the exact way he has always wanted to live it. He doesn't regret a single thing. What is wrong then?

Many nights, he concludes that his daughter is to blame for his unhappiness and wishes she had moved to Rio and married the Brazilian forestry student with the curly hair, the wispy moustache and the obsession with Elis Regina. Some nights he blames his ex-wife—and then he blames Finland (for reasons that will soon become clear), then Norway, then Sweden—and all of Scandinavia until he finally dismisses the whole problem and eventually falls asleep. In the morning, he shakes himself awake, rises slowly to his feet, and tries to forget about his unhappiness. Sometimes he succeeds.

On the intermittent days when he believes he is approaching something akin to normal and feels almost well, he chats to his neighbor down the hall, an old man, once an incurable meth addict, now virtually catatonic. This man sits in a wooden chair placed just outside his door, moving his fingers incessantly as if typing a letter or playing the piano. This is how he spends his time between lunch and dinner, and this is when the professor comes to visit him. It can't really be called a *visit*— no reasonable person would call it that—but the professor thinks of it in this way and believes he is doing the man a service.

Usually around three o'clock or so, the professor approaches him, looks down at him, and says, "I'm not supposed to be here, you know." Or, "This is all a mistake." Or, "I live in a big house, you know, with an oak tree." Or, "My daughter is responsible for my incarceration." Or, "Did you know owls may befriend small cats?" Or, "Can you play the "Emperor Waltz"?"

Sometimes, he can't resist the impulse to lecture and goes on and on about Hume. His neighbor stares up at him, dislodges his false teeth with his tongue, flutters his fingers in the air, then closes his eyes, and covers his ears with his hands. And the professor walks away, feeling that he has helped this man by giving him a rare opportunity for social interaction.

On bad nights, when he can't sleep at all, the professor

recalls—no, it is more like he is summoned to witness—moments and episodes in his life, and he tries to answer how and why he has ended up here. Never, ever—even before his studies in philosophy—did he ever really *choose* anything. As a child, he did whatever he was told to do. Never rebelled, never questioned. He went to the university of his parents' choice and became a student of philosophy because he couldn't think of anything else to do. He became a professor of philosophy because that was the obvious path to take. He married his wife because it was what she wanted. He wrote books because his department head told him he should do so.

At every turn in his life, he simply stumbled into whatever plausible path appeared before him. And then, when he delved into the ideas of d'Holbach, Ginet, and others, he realized that there was nothing abnormal about this. This is what humans do. Always. We never really choose. We simply follow prescribed procedures dictated by social conditioning and predetermined biological paths. Free will does not exist. And we shouldn't pretend that it does. The only honest way to live would be to do absolutely nothing, like Diogenes or Bartleby.

And from this Eureka moment on, when he put down d'Holbach's *The System of Nature*, marched out into the street, took a deep breath, and felt, for the first time, utterly free and alive, he lived his life according to the principle which he now firmly believed: he renounced his will. Not that he *chose* to renounce it—no no, he simply ended up doing so, he told himself. In the face of any decision it appeared he had to make, he consciously allowed himself to fall into a default position.

It drove his wife crazy. Fine. So be it. He didn't blame her for the Finnish construction worker she took up with on the sly.

Nor for the divorce. It happened most amicably, and he accepted it all—including unfair alimony payments, grossly inflated by his wife's dependence on exotic nutritionists, an overpriced psychotherapist she'd been seeing for fifteen years, and her essential need for a house in Rosedale. *Essential? What the*—?

And what did that construction worker have that he didn't have? He looked like a Nazi and probably was one—what a sad loss of a human being—but no no, it was all alright and perfectly amicable in the end. They even had dinner together once. He drank too much Aquavit and called the construction worker a Prussian nihilist and a thug—or was it a lout? But never mind. That was a long time ago, and it's alright now, perfectly amicable. And all of this is beside the point. Back to the question. Which is:

Why, why, why the depression, the anxiety, the panic, the Ativan, the vodka, the cockatoos, and domesticated donkeys—the descent into all the worst habits he could possibly fall prey to. Why, why, why? Good question. Bad habits—are they predetermined? Yes, yes, obviously, they are. They are *not* his fault. There is a neurological cause for them, namely perniciously malignant brain chemistry. And nothing he can do about it. So. Ok. Fine.

But the problem is he doesn't feel *good* about any of this. He doesn't want to be here. He really doesn't. More to the point: he doesn't want to have ended up here. There is something very wrong—and he doesn't believe that any kind of "deliberative thought" is going to get him out of this. Nothing can get him out of this—nothing. This is where he finds himself on his bad nights, which always lead to worse mornings and catastrophic afternoons.

One awful morning, brooding on the question of how he ended up here, he spends three hours hashing through his belief in the non-existence of free will. He is having terrible doubts—perhaps the thing exists in some way. But no. It's impossible. Has he missed something? He goes back and forth and around in circles, pacing in his room like he used to do in his lectures.

By the afternoon, his turmoil is threatening to rise into a rage. He marches over to his neighbor, stands in front of him, leans down, and says, "So. What do you believe in? *Eh?* What is the principle by which you lead your life? Do you believe in free will? *Do you?*" And he leans in close until his nose is inches from his neighbor's face. His neighbor is asleep. "Let me tell you this, my friend—and it's the truth—free will does not exist. We have seen the neurological evidence; we have seen the biological evidence. It simply does. Not. Exist. But—listen to me, listen to me! It doesn't exist—but here's the catch—you'd fucking well better believe it fucking well *does* exist, *do you hear me? If you want to live an acceptable life, you'd better believe in it, man, and that's my advice to you. I hope you remember that.*"

His neighbor drools into the neck of his T-shirt, and the professor shuffles back to his room, leaning against the wall and sliding along it. He sits on the edge of his bed and stares out the window. He is shocked by his own words—his anger. In this moment of lucidity, and just before he is given his meds, he considers the meaning of what he has just said—the aporia he has brought himself to—that he must believe in something that does not exist in order to continue to live his life in an acceptable way. Could this be so? Could he have been wrong—all this time? Could it be that free will is some kind of a *real thing*? An irradicable human value? No no no no. It goes against every principle in his life and strains every cell in his prefrontal cortex. Causes him a sharp pain in his chest. It is impossible. Free will does not exist. We know it cannot exist. And so why, oh, why must he believe in it to live a good life?

The answer that surfaces from somewhere—who knows where—horrifies him: because he has not lived well. He is nothing less than the living proof of the experiment. In his life, and on the question of how to live a good life, he has defaulted. Now he can see that there *were* choices he could have made—he could have been kinder to his wife, for one—but he didn't make those choices. He didn't make any choices. He simply allowed himself to free fall into the worst version of himself. He was— was he? *Irresponsible?* No. But yes but no but yes—he has wasted every moment of his life. So then. It must be true: to carry on at all—to live a decent life—he must believe in this thing—this *free will*—that does not exist. Nausea occurs when he considers the unavoidable conclusion of this chain of thought: if he is to believe in free will, he might as well believe in *God*, convert to Christianity, become an Evangelist or an Orthodox Jew. Why not?

This contradiction—this double bind—torments him so much that when the nurse comes into his room at four, she finds him sitting on the floor, twisting his bed sheet into a rope. Gently she takes the sheet away from him and sits beside him on the floor.

"What's wrong?" she says.

"It doesn't make sense," he says. "I can't make it make sense, you see. I can't even *ask* it to make sense. The thing is locked horns, an unsolvable impasse. And if there's no sense to it, then there's no sense in the way I've lived my life to this point. It's worthless and meaningless. And wrong. So you see."

"Yes, I do see," she says. "You are in a good place."

"What can you possibly mean by that?"

"Confusion and doubt are the beginnings of true change."

"Who told you that?"

"No one."

"*Really?*"

"Well, no one on this earth."

"Ah. I see," he says quietly.

"The Son of God loves you."

"Oh really," he says.

He sits cross-legged, elbows on knees, head hanging, covering his face with his hands. "Fucking hell," he mutters through his fingers. He shakes his head from side to side, gripping his ears as if he'd like to twist his head off his neck. Then he sobs into his hands.

There is one thing he hasn't thought of that he thinks of now: maybe the truth is he's an irresponsible shit. Maybe that's just who he is. Why should he assume that a belief in free will would make any difference at all? It's quite possible that even if he believed in it passionately all his life, he'd still be an irresponsible shit. He'd just be an irresponsible shit who believes in free will—and that would be the only difference. But— perhaps it is not a good thing to be an irresponsible shit? No no. There is no good or bad about it. He didn't give birth to himself. This is who he is. So be it.

He stops sobbing, wipes his face, turns slowly to the nurse, and smiles a wide and hopeful smile. "Do you have any Oreo-chip ice cream here?" he says. "I wouldn't mind having some if you have it."

She stands, folds up the sheet, and helps him to his feet. "I'll see what we can do," she says and hands him a small glass of water and a tiny pill on a plate.

* * *

In years to come, his students will forget about their beloved professor, or they might wonder whatever happened to him. They might assume he will still be teaching, but he will not. Just two years after his release from the Fairview Rehab Centre, he will take early retirement, abandon his house, and move to the Dominican Republic, where he will live alone in a small cottage the color of strawberry ice cream with lime green shutters at the edge of a dusty road.

Inside the house will be many small bottles of Ativan on the kitchen table, many empty vodka bottles strewn across the floor, many birds flying back and forth outside his open door. There will even be a small ice cream stand not far from his house, open in the afternoons. They will not have Oreo-chip ice cream there. The only flavor they will have will be vanilla. This will be a terrible disappointment to him, but after a time, he will come to accept it as an inescapable truth of his reality.

Every so often, his daughter will send him an email recommending a new vitamin. Sometimes he will reply, and sometimes he won't.

And we can be absolutely certain that all these things will happen in just this way and no other. Because, well, you know.

* * *

This story first appeared in the After Dinner Conversation—July 2023 issue.

Discussion Questions

1. Do you believe, as the professor does, that there is no free will and that all our choices are predetermined? What is the reason/basis for your opinion, and how does it affect your life choices?

2. The professor believes, at one point in the story, that his miserable life was caused by his lack of belief in free will. Do you agree? Is there another reason the professor is unhappy?

3. Is it possible for people who think deeply about these kinds of things to be happy? Is it harder to be happy when you are a deep thinker about life? If so, does this mean we shouldn't think too deeply about life?

4. What would you say to the professor while he is in the hospital? What, if anything, do you think he needs from others, or to know, to heal?

5. At the end of the story, the professor concludes that believing in a lie, free will, is the best way to be happy. Do you agree? He additionally concludes that intentional self-deception (*like about free will*) creates a happier life. Do you agree? If so, what knowing lies do you embrace for the sake of your own happiness and why?

* * *

T a p s

Paul Hilding

* * *

I am alone, standing on the crumbling back steps of the old church, my trumpet by my side in my right hand. The church cemetery, dotted with countless rows of neatly arranged headstones, descends gradually towards the slate grey sea. It is a raw blustery day in mid-April. The first buds have appeared on the wild roses that have overgrown the cemetery wall, and on the storm-blasted stand of oak trees beyond. A single white sail is visible offshore. The damp salt air carries a faint smell of decay, of seaweed and debris washed up on distant beaches. Far below, a small group of mourners is gathered by an open grave.

He and I were about the same age, from neighboring towns, but had never met. Still, I knew well the difficult choice he had been forced to make fifty years ago, as he graduated high school and began planning his life. It was the same choice I had faced, at about the same time. It was the same choice faced by the three others I had played for in the past year, dozens of others over past decades. All of them had chosen to serve. All except me.

Someone from VFW called me a few days ago. They know I play for Vietnam vets. This also is my choice. But, no matter how many times I play, it seems I can never make up for that other choice I made, so long ago.

The newspaper story had been respectful but short. He had been a good student and an athlete, a star wide receiver in high school. Wounded at Lang Vei. Bronze Star. Purple Heart. Two weeks ago a road crew had found him under a bridge, most of his worldly possessions in a rusty shopping cart hidden in the brush nearby.

As always, I needed to know more. By now, after so many, I had a set routine. As soon as I received the call from VFW, I Google-searched the name. I tracked down family and friends. I learned as much as I could about where and when they had served, battles they had fought, what they had done after the war. But mostly, I tried to figure out why. Why had they chosen to serve? I felt like I had to know before I could play at the service, before I could even attempt to honor the sacrifice. The sacrifice I had avoided making.

From my investigations of the others, I learned that some had believed in the war, but that many thought it was a mistake. They hadn't bought the bullshit about falling dominoes, about fighting for democracy in a godforsaken jungle on the other side of the world. They had gone anyhow, even though there had been other choices.

What about this one, the one under the bridge? His name was Daniel. Such a promising life ahead of him. Why had he gone?

As I began gathering information about Daniel, and

reading about the Battle of Lang Vei, I soon realized his funeral would not be like the others. As difficult as they had been, for me Daniel's would be by far the most wrenching. It was not just because of the horrific accounts of the battle I located online. No, there was something else. There was a coincidence, a brutal personal connection. The deeper I dug into Daniel's story, the more excruciating the pain I felt. I doubted I would be able to play at the funeral. But I also realized I could never live with myself if I did not.

Lang Vei had been a small Special Forces outpost deep in the jungle in the far north of South Vietnam. It was one of North Vietnam's first targets during the Tet Offensive, the North's all-out attempt to win the war in early 1968. On February 6, 1968, two dozen Green Berets and a few hundred South Vietnamese and Lao soldiers were directly in the path of three battalions of North Vietnamese infantry and a dozen Soviet-made tanks.

The defenders put up a fierce fight, taking out five of the twelve tanks. But the base was quickly overrun and, as eight of the surviving Green Berets fell back to the reinforced concrete command bunker, they learned that their repeated requests for reinforcements from Khe Sanh, a large American Marine base just six miles away, had been denied.

Somehow, they managed to hold out in the bunker for fifteen hours, as the North Vietnamese tried to dislodge them with tear gas, fragmentation grenades, point-blank tank fire and, finally, several bricks of C-4 in the ventilation system. All but one of the Green Berets were badly injured by gunfire, shrapnel and the shock waves from the repeated explosions in the enclosed space of the bunker. But, under cover of long-delayed American air strikes, seven of the eight managed to escape.

I also found online the cruel footnote to the story. After months of defending Khe Sanh against the North Vietnamese attack, after American planes had dropped more than 100,000 tons of bombs on enemy forces in the area, after thousands of American troops had been killed or wounded, the North Vietnamese assault was finally defeated. However, only two months later, in June of 1968, America's war planners decided that Khe Sanh no longer served America's military strategy and all troops were withdrawn. Khe Sanh was abandoned.

* * *

As it happened, February 6, 1968 was also an important day in my own life. On the very day that Daniel and his comrades were trying to escape that firestorm of machine gun fire, artillery rounds and Russian tanks, I was also planning an escape. I had spent that morning at home, packing a suitcase and backpack and had then jammed them, along with my trumpet case, into the trunk of my first car, a battered old Volkswagen Beetle with bald tires and a cracked windshield.

I had already decided that the Vietnam War was both stupid and immoral. My parents and nearly all my friends agreed with me. I had just read, cover to cover, the newly-published "Manual for Draft-Age Immigrants to Canada."

Later that day I had a final, somber dinner with my parents. We went over my options one more time. Yes, the war was wrong. But what was the right thing to do? Serve anyway, be complicit in senseless killing, and possibly lose my own life? Resist, join the anti-war protests, and end up in prison with a criminal record that would last a lifetime? Or escape to Canada, and risk never being able to return home? As before, we came to the same conclusion. Canada was only 200 miles away. It was the best of three lousy choices.

Dad quietly reviewed with me the procedures for requesting permanent immigration status, job leads he had managed to get through family friends in Montreal, college classes he would help me pay for, and plans for my return home "after the war." I remember the brave smile on my mother's face, her tearful reassurance about how wonderful Canada would be. After a sleepless night and goodbye hugs in the icy driveway the next morning, I started driving north on mostly deserted roads across a grey winter landscape.

I did not return home for nine years, after the amnesty. I had enough credits from courses in Canada that I was able to quickly finish my music degree and find a job teaching at a nearby high school. After a short, childless marriage, I moved into a one-bedroom apartment near the school and busied myself with my job, conducting both the high school band and chorus and giving voice and instrumental lessons.

More than anything, the enthusiasm and joy of my students inspired and sustained me. By diving deep into this work that I loved I felt like I was mostly succeeding in controlling my dark thoughts about the war. For a time, I even persuaded myself that playing taps at funerals was a just penance and that eventually, after enough funerals, perhaps I would feel like I had paid my dues.

For most of those years I considered it a blessing that the military draft had ended and that my students would never be forced to choose between going to war, going to jail, or going to Canada. It was only shortly before I retired that I began to have second thoughts. One day, during a lunchtime rehearsal, the assistant principal stopped by and asked one of the band members, a giggly redhead named Jan, to come with him to the office. We learned later that Jan's father was one of four American servicemen killed in an ambush earlier that week in Africa, in the country of Niger.

The main emotion at school seemed to be disbelief, even more than sadness or grief. No one even knew where Niger was, let alone why Americans were fighting a war there.

Shortly after, on one of the few evenings when I was not busy preparing for classes, or practicing my own instruments, I caught myself questioning everything I thought I believed about the draft. Yes, Jan's father had enlisted. There was no law that had required him to serve. But, I thought to my own surprise, would it be better if there was a draft? What if every family in America had to sit down at the dinner table, as my parents had with me during the Vietnam War, and really think about whether or not a war in Southeast Asia, or in West Africa, or on the Arabian Peninsula, was necessary to "defend" the country? Would America find other ways to solve its problems if everyone's child was potential cannon fodder?

* * *

It was not hard to locate Daniel's younger sister Anna. She still lived in the neighboring town where she and Daniel had grown up. The number for her landline popped up with a white pages search. She answered on the first ring and sounded pleased to meet with me after I explained I would be playing at his funeral the next day.

On the drive to Anna's house, I realized I was approaching the bridge above the area where they had found Daniel's body. I started wondering about Daniel's final days. I decided I needed to stop.

The bridge spanned a small creek flowing through a weedy concrete culvert. I left my car in the rear parking lot of an abandoned strip mall and climbed down a muddy slope. Under the bridge I soon found the scattered remains of a campsite. Pieces of cardboard and a torn tarp littered the underbrush. An old folding cot, one leg missing, rested upside down in the weeds. Someone had kicked the blackened stones from a small fire ring down towards the creek.

After looking closely in the damp soil, I located the marks where the legs of the cot had rested before the campsite had been disturbed. Close by, I stumbled over a flat rock hidden in the weeds. The rock seemed out of place and I lifted a corner. Underneath, in a shallow hole, was a black trash bag. I unknotted the bag and found several bottles of prescription medications with Daniel's name. Also in the bag was a headlamp, a few coins, and an old cigarette carton duct-taped shut.

When I pulled the tape off the carton, a Purple Heart slid into my hand, smooth and cold as a headstone. I stood motionless for a long time, looking down at the medal. A light rain had begun to fall, the patter of raindrops joining the chorus of rushing water in the creek and the far-off sounds of traffic. But also in that moment I imagined I heard a quiet voice, as if Daniel's medal was speaking to me about his sacrifice. And suffering. About the profound importance of choices. I felt a numbness and a weariness as old doubts, the doubts that had haunted me for fifty years, descended like a dark fog.

The final item in the trash bag was a thick weathered book, so worn and water-stained that I could barely make out its title, *The Collected Dialogues of Plato*. Many of the pages were dog-eared, with text either underlined in ink or highlighted with a yellow marker. The margins were crammed with handwritten notes, arrows and other symbols, most unreadable.

I was late for my meeting with Anna. But, somehow, I knew I needed to spend a few minutes with this book before I would be ready to talk to her.

There was a leather bookmark still in place near the front, in the "Crito" dialogue. I opened the book to that page and caught my breath as I read the highlighted text.

Look at it in this way. Suppose that while we were preparing to run away from here – or however you would describe it – the laws and constitution of Athens were to come and confront us and ask this question: 'Now, Socrates, what are you proposing to do? Can you deny that by this act which you are contemplating you intend, so far as you have the power, to destroy us, the laws, and the whole state as well? Do you imagine that a nation can continue to exist and not be turned upside down, if the legal judgments which are pronounced in it have no force and are nullified and destroyed by private persons?

Once again, I stood motionless for a long moment. Another of Daniel's prized possessions seemed to be speaking to me. Finally, I managed to flip back a few pages to the short introduction which explained that the "Crito" dialogue dealt with the aftermath of the trial of Socrates, after an Athenian jury had unjustly sentenced him to death. As the dialogue begins, Socrates is in jail awaiting execution. His friend Crito had been allowed to visit and is urging Socrates to let Crito bribe the jailer so Socrates can escape to another country.

Even after twenty-five centuries, the scorn in Socrates' response was unmistakable: "run away from here – or however you would describe it..." Socrates had flatly rejected his "Canada" option. Having failed to persuade his fellow citizens of the error of their judgment, he chose to remain in jail, awaiting execution, rather than flee his beloved Athens.

As with my own countrymen who had chosen to serve, I needed to understand why. I spent another half hour reading the full dialogue before putting the book, along with the rest of Daniel's possessions, back in the bag and climbing up the embankment to my car.

* * *

Anna lived in a small white bungalow on a quiet side street, just a few miles from the bridge. The yard and house were neatly kept. The rain shower had stopped and sunlight was slanting through the clouds, reflecting off the still-wet sidewalk and porch and lighting up the red geraniums in her front window boxes. I parked the car and, with an old napkin I found under the seat, tried to wipe the mud off the plastic bag. As I got out of the car with the bag, I saw Anna waiting at the open front door.

"I'm so sorry I'm late," I said as I hurried up the sidewalk, still brushing at the bag with the napkin. "I'm John. This belongs to Daniel. I just found it, under..."

"The bridge," she said quietly. "I, I have been trying to talk myself into going there." She was tall and thin, with dark distracted eyes framed by bookish glasses and short greying hair. She appeared to be in her early 60s, perhaps ten years younger than her brother. "We used to play there when we were kids. We made forts and..." She looked away suddenly, blinking her eyes. "I didn't even know he was back in town until they told me they had found him."

"No need to go. It's very muddy from the rain," I said. "I think I found everything. This was hidden in the brush." I handed her the bag.

"Thank you so much. Please, please, come in. Would you like some coffee?"

I nodded and peeled off my shoes at the door, following her into the house. She gestured for me to sit in one of two wicker chairs facing each other in the small sunlit living room. There was a pot of coffee and some mugs on a low glass table between the chairs.

Anna placed the bag on the table and began untying the knot, heedless of the dried mud flaking off the bag. "Thank you so much for agreeing to play at his funeral," she said, looking down at the bag. "There really aren't that many people that will be there, but it will mean so much to those of us who can make it. He lost touch with his friends, everyone actually, especially after he went off his meds. You know, he was okay for a couple years after he came back. He went to college and later he was selling real estate in Chicago but then he had some kind of a breakdown..."

I nodded. "I'm so sorry. I hope this isn't too painful, but I wanted to know more about Daniel. For the service. It helps me..."

"He was a musician also," Anna said, a thin smile on her lips. "He played guitar, and he sang. He had such a sweet voice." The bag was now open and she carefully examined the bottles of medication before putting them down on the table.

Next, she pulled out the cigarette carton. The Purple Heart fell onto the floor and she quickly reached down to pick it up. There was a long silence as she turned it over in her hand.

Finally, she placed the medal on the table as well and pulled the Plato book from the bag. "I think this was one of his textbooks," she said slowly as she looked it over. "College was so hard for him. He started when he got back, just a few weeks after the massacre at My Lai. The students were protesting. They carried signs that said 'baby killers.' He never fit in."

"It must have been very difficult for him," I said. "What was he studying?"

"He was a philosophy major. Even after all these years, I remember a long talk one evening while he was still in college. He seemed so excited, so hopeful. It's the last time I remember him like that. He mentioned a professor, a retired Marine, who was helping him in one of the courses, a Plato seminar," she said, pointing to the book. "He said that, with the help of his professor, he was figuring some things out, that there were so many surprising parallels, even across thousands of years."

I leaned forward. "Do you know what he meant by that?"

She paused, as if considering whether to continue. "He told me he felt a very strong connection with Socrates. It was almost... weird." She looked down at the medal. "He talked like they had been friends, as if they had spent time together. Socrates had also served in the army and survived a war. Socrates was also a social outcast. And, most important for Daniel, Socrates had also loved his country, or perhaps the ideal of his country."

She reached over to fill my coffee cup and then filled her own, holding it in her lap. "I remember he also said that, at its height, Athens, like America, was the world's greatest democracy. And the most arrogant, embroiled in endless wars."

"So, he was not in favor of the Vietnam War?" I asked, hoping the tone of my voice sounded neutral.

"Well, he did decide to enlist," she said, the thin smile

returning briefly. "Our father had fought in World War II and I think he wanted Dad to be proud of him. But Dan definitely had his doubts about Vietnam, even then." She paused, then looked directly at me. "What about you? What did you do?"

"I, I went to Canada," I said. I felt my face reddening. There was an awkward silence. I shifted in my chair. "I studied music."

"I see," said Anna. After another pause she jumped up suddenly. "Hey. Let me show you a picture of Daniel. This one is from before the war." It was Daniel's prom picture. He looked pretty much like I had imagined. Tall, athletic, he had soft brown eyes and a big goofy grin on his face. Dressed in a black tuxedo, he had his arm around a smiling blond girl with a light blue gown that matched her eyes. "Her name was Carolynn, Daniel's first girlfriend. I was seven. I thought she was so beautiful."

Anna continued talking, about the prom, about their upbringing, about their father's expectations, but I wasn't really listening anymore. Instead, I was again wondering about Daniel. Did he also have a lifelong debate with himself about the war? Like Socrates, he had confronted "the laws and constitution" of the country he loved, and had chosen to obey. After reading the "Crito", had he found any solace?

Anna seemed to sense that I was distracted and she thanked me again as we said overly hasty goodbyes. It was late afternoon, and I headed to the old church to practice the trumpet, another routine I had gotten into long ago. I needed to prepare for tomorrow. But also, over the years, I discovered it worked even better than alcohol to calm me, to quiet inner voices. More than ever, I needed my music fix today.

By the time I arrived a storm had kicked up and a cold, heavy rain was falling. I hurried to the side door.

The church was not much to look at. The steeple had blown off in another storm many years before and was never replaced by the frugal New England congregation, so all that was left above the sanctuary was a stub for the bell tower. The sagging sanctuary itself was more than two hundred years old and the peeling white paint on its weathered wood siding was badly in need of care. Someone had recently painted the enormous front doors an almost neon orange, perhaps a vain attempt to attract attention and new members.

I heard the rumble of a pipe organ above the shrill wind even before I stepped inside. The sanctuary was dark, the only light coming from the long row of tall, thin stained-glass windows that ran the length of the building on both sides. It smelled of old wood, dusty hymnals and candle wax, of generations of Christmas Eves and baptisms and funerals.

In the dim light, behind a simple altar, I could make out the massive gleaming pipes of the organ, the gold ornamentation on the supporting struts, the rich wood finish of the keyboard frame and backing panels. The rest of the sanctuary was unadorned. The pews were bare pine benches. The tile floor was cracked and stained with age.

The organist, a slight man in his forties with silver-rimmed glasses, was pounding out a Bach fugue, filling the sanctuary with a rich, resonant wall of sound, the bass so powerful it shook the floor and seemed to press on my chest. I felt like I was caught inside a thundering whirlwind, like I was having trouble breathing. Images of a brutal jungle war began swirling in my head.

The organist finished and started putting away his music. I had met him at some of the previous funerals. He saw me standing in the back of the church.

"Wow, beautiful," I managed, trying to catch my breath.

He thanked me, then asked with a sad smile, "So, are you playing again, John?"

"Yeah, tomorrow. Daniel Adams. I think he was in the choir when he was a kid."

"A little before my time," said the organist. "I read about him in the paper. Someone told me he had a voice like an angel."

"They found him two weeks ago," I heard myself say. "Under the Grove Street Bridge."

"I'll be there," he said, a look of concern on his face as he glanced up at me. "Take care of yourself John."

After he left, I opened my trumpet case. The trumpet lay cushioned in dark blue velvet, the flawless brass finish reflecting the red, yellow and orange light streaming through the stained glass. I had never been a believer, but had long ago discovered an emotional and spiritual connection to my music. On some of the darkest days of my life, music had provided comfort and even joy. These feelings, I had long imagined, must be close to religious experience.

Even before I touched the trumpet, I could feel my mind beginning to quiet, the stress beginning to ebb, my heart rate slowing. As always, I picked it up carefully with a white handkerchief to avoid damaging the finish. I walked to the front of the church.

Years ago, when I was learning to play, an instructor had told me to visualize each note as a pearl with smooth rounded edges, circular pearls for short notes, oval pearls for longer notes. I had worked hard to follow his advice, but somehow it had always seemed too clinical, too limiting. Back then, the sound of my horn in practice rooms had seemed pale, almost muted. I had always thought my trumpet was capable of so much more.

As I got older and started playing in auditoriums and concert halls, I noticed the tone became richer and deeper. But there was something special about the sound in that old church, a resonance and an undertone that seemed to rise as much from the old timbers as from the horn itself. Or, as I sometimes imagined, from the ghostly echoes of two centuries of prayer.

As usual, I warmed up playing notes in the lower and middle range. Then, from memory, I started playing a favorite solo from "Summertime." I closed my eyes as the storm raged outside. A new vision started to form. I saw warm, smooth flowing gold. It was a magical place, a place I did not want to leave.

Finally, I began playing more in the upper register and eventually got to my favorite, a Vivaldi trumpet concerto. This time when I closed my eyes, brilliant flashes of silver replaced the gold. I played through the entire piece two or three times, mesmerized by the explosions of light. Again, I could not bring myself to break the spell.

My cell phone buzzed and I looked down to see a text message from Anna: "Hi John. I just wanted you to know that Daniel would never have questioned your choice. Only his own. I'll see you tomorrow."

* * *

I watch as the casket is lowered slowly into the ground. I picture a smiling high school boy in a black tuxedo on prom night, a boy who wanted to please his father. Not a mentally ill homeless man. I tell myself that the February 6 coincidence has nothing to do with whether I made the right choice. I tell myself that what happened to Daniel that day was not my fault.

Anna is standing by herself, near the head of the grave. She looks lonely and frail in the gusting wind. She pauses for a moment and then bends forward, gently placing the book and the Purple Heart on top of the coffin just before it disappears below ground.

The pastor signals to me. I lift the trumpet from my side and press the cold mouthpiece tight to my lips. This time there is no warm building enveloping the sound. No flowing gold or flashes of silver. Just pearls, pale as the morning sky, descending the hillside to the small group by the grave, before returning to the sea. I close my eyes as I hold the long final note.

* * *

This story first appeared in the After Dinner Conversation—July 2021 issue.

Discussion Questions

1. John, the narrator, felt he had two choices; to flee to Canada, or to deny the draft and join the protests. Were those his only choices? If you were in his position, what would you have done, and why?

2. If John feels the Vietnam War was an unjust war, why do you think he feels so bad about fleeing to Canada? Why does he feel the need to do penance by playing military funerals?

3. In "Crito," the question is asked, "Do you imagine that a nation can continue to exist...if the legal judgments which are pronounced in it have no force and are nullified and destroyed by private persons?" What does this statement mean, and do you agree with the idea it is putting forward?

4. Are those who serve in the military and fight in wars they personally feel are unjust, heroes or cowards? Which is the "bravest" choice, to flee the country, to protest the laws and be arrested, or to serve in a conflict you believe is wrong?

5. Does loving, and serving, your country include supporting it even when you disagree with what it is doing? How do you know which things you disagree with to do anyway, and which you have a duty to disobey? What would be an example of a silly law you obey anyway?

* * *

They Got Their Show

Garrett Davis

* * *

It is midnight in Ponderosa and Nick Velasquez can't sleep. The public doesn't want him to sleep. It's been like this ever since it hit all the big streaming platforms. The viewers stay up bingeing and he... well, he has been bingeing in his own way. With a bottle of tequila in one hand and a lit joint in the other, Nick wanders from room to room like a ghost in his own house. He shuffles through indents made in the living room carpet. Depressions from the furniture his *esposa*, Marcella, took with her when she left. *Can't look at my eyes without seeing our little girl.* Nick pulls on the joint, its coal shifting from a deep cherry red to bright yellow in the darkness. He exhales a plume of smoke and walks down the hall, his sobriety trailing behind him. *And just when things were getting back to normal.* He'd gotten a job at a local taxi company, found a support group with minimal *woo-woo*, hell he'd even gotten Marcella on the phone once or twice but then the docuseries hit Netflix.

He's been circling the house all evening, like water going

down the drain, each revolution getting smaller and smaller bringing him down inevitably to a single point. His daughter's room. Everything is, more or less, as Carmen left it; Notorious B.I.G. posters, a half-made bed and her diary open to a blank page dated June 17th 1995. Stumbling into the room, he squares off with the closet. A four-year-old Carmen wouldn't sleep if the closet door was left open at night. She got scared that if it were left open, monsters from the dark could just walk on in. So being a good daddy, Nick made a big show of closing the doors and threatening any would-be monsters inside. It became a nightly ritual until at fifteen, her embarrassed protests hit home. Nick takes a swig from the bottle and wipes his mouth using the back of his hand. He'd asked her once why the monsters didn't simply push the door open.

"Daddy," she had said, "the handle is on the outside."

Swaying slightly, it seems to Nick that the evil behind those bifold closet doors is almost palpable. It might be the drugs or maybe it's the liquor but he swears he can feel pressure built up behind those doors. He sees darkness leaking out from underneath and marvels at the strength of those flimsy tarnished brass hinges. Putting the bottle down, he extends a shaking hand.

"Don't do this," he whispers to himself.

The doors open, revealing stacks upon stacks of banker's boxes. They're piled floor to ceiling, each one labeled in fat black ink: **1995**. He takes a shot of tequila for each box he brings to the living room. Marcella had been nice enough to leave him an old reclining chair and he had since bought a secondhand television. So bathed in blue TV light, Nick gets to work. He organizes statements, arranges and rearranges glossy eight by ten photographs and rereads old newspaper clippings. Back in 1995 Carmen and a local boy Benjie left the house to rent a movie from Blockbuster. They did this every weekend. Nick would give Carmen twenty dollars and she and Benjie would walk the three blocks to the video store. But on June 17th, 1995, they never returned.

The docuseries plays in the background. *When did I put that on?* It details what they call *shady police work* and *circumstantial evidence*. It claims that the country has put an innocent man on death row. Nick glances at his masterpiece, laid out just as he remembers it; each document linked by a thread of red string, and they all lead to Benjie. He'd cut Benjie's photo out of one of Carmen's old yearbooks; they'd gone to school together. Benjie is fat in the photo, his face pitted with acne. Every grad class has one fat loser that no one likes—no one but Carmen that is. Nick puffs on his joint in contemplation. He never understood what made them such fast friends. He finds his answer in another memory, something Marcella once told him. Her words hang in the forefront of his mind and he's so high he swears he can actually hear her say it.

"She wants to fix him," Marcella had said, "she just doesn't know that yet."

"Well she's certainly not in it for his brains," Nick says aloud, reliving the conversation in real time. "If I had a line-up of potential school shooters... I'd pick that sad little *puto* nine out of ten times."

The public, however, didn't seem to feel that way. Benjie is on the screen now, much older and less ruddy in the face. Nick suspects he's wearing makeup for the shot. The lighting is good — the angle flattering — he almost looks handsome. *Like lipstick on a pig.*

"Did you kill Carmen Velasquez?" the interviewer asks.

"No," Benjie answers. "Why, uh, why's everyone still asking that? I've been in here nearly, uh, twenty years and my story hasn't changed. And do you want to know why?"

"Why?" the reporter asks.

"Cause it's the truth. I ain't never hurt a fly in my life."

When Benjie says this, Nick hears the pings; likes and retweets being sent out from the viewers. He picks them up like radio waves on teeth fillings. They sound like the bells and whistles on an old pinball machine. *I'm on a whole 'nother frequency, hombre!* That's when it falls apart. He sees the mistake in his careful plotting on the floor.

Benjie and Carmen were found three blocks from the Blockbuster Video in an alley. Benjie was unconscious and Carmen... both of them were covered in her blood. The autopsy report says her throat had been slit from behind, but that the cut hadn't been deep enough to be fatal. The attacker — probably in a panic — had bludgeoned her to death with a cinderblock that had been used as a doorstop. The knife was in Benjie's unconscious hand when the police arrived. Benjie never denied that the knife was his. His toxicology came back clean. There was nothing to explain his blackout. The detail that Nick had overlooked all this time was the pendant of St. Christopher hanging around Carmen's neck. The patron saint of protection, a birthday gift in case Daddy wasn't around to deal with the monsters. It is missing in the crime scene photo. Benjie had been searched and it wasn't on his person at the time. Nor could it be found in the subsequent combing of the crime scene. *Could someone else have taken it? Would that prove someone else was there?*

A phone rings, yanking Nick from his thoughts and making him jump. The call display says: Dispatch. Everyone in the company is required to be on call once a week. That meant if some suit and tie needs a lift to the airport at three A.M., you saddle up and ride. Tonight isn't his night, he's sure of it, and so he lets it go to voicemail. The display goes dark momentarily before dancing and lighting up again. Nick picks up, opening his mouth to set free a string of expletives only to find his brain hadn't yet finished translating them to English. What does come out is a sort of involuntary muffled burp.

"Listen Nicky, before you fly off the handle," the Dispatcher says, "I want you to know that I know it's late. Not only that," he continues, "but I know that it's not your night tonight. I got a call you might find interesting."

There's a beeping as Dispatch patches two lines together. When it's done, Nick hears a recording taken for quality assurance purposes. The recording starts with an automated message from the incoming caller. It says:

"You have a collect call from Ponderosa Penitentiary. To accept charges and connect, please press the pound key." A button is pressed and the line crackles as it is transferred.

"Ponderosa Taxi, how may I direct your call?" the recording says.

"Uh, hello?" comes an unmistakable voice from the other side, "I was wondering if I, uh, could schedule a pick up?"

Suddenly, it feels hard to breathe. Nick's throat feels as though he's been gargling gravel and sleet. He knows that voice, has heard that voice in his haunted dreams for nearly thirty years — Benjie.

"What's the address?" asks Dispatch.

"Well, uh, I get out tomorrow and I — will you pick people up from the prison or is that weird?"

"We'll pick you up but we won't break you out."

Benjie laughs. The thought of anything resembling joy coming from his piggy snout makes Nick's blood boil. He almost hangs up right then and there, he wants to throw the phone and watch the cheap plastic explode into a million little pieces, but he doesn't. Instead he snuffs out the joint in a crystal ashtray and brings the liquor bottle to his lips. Nothing comes out. The worm clinks against the bottleneck.

"Nicky? Are you still there?"

"Yeah," Nick says. "I'm here."

"So, what do you say?"

"I say you got some goddamn giant bull balls. Did you dream this up on your own? Who put this *loca* idea into your thick skull?"

"Whoa, Nick buddy," he replies. "I don't know what you think I'm suggesting but whatever it is, I ain't! I just figured that maybe you'd want to see him. Maybe apologize, get that — uh, whatcha call it — document?"

Nick sits down in his recliner. His head hurts something fierce. Pinching the bridge of his nose, he says, "It's denouement, not document; a nice neat ending."

"Well, well, well... look at the big brain on you! Listen, his gran passed away while he's been locked up. Give him a lift to her old house. Get whatever is on your chest out and in the open, and say your goodbyes. Hell, he'll probably skip town after! I know I would. The whole world knowing my story... I'd get out."

Nick stares at the pictures lined up on the floor; all the papers, the bits of string. Reminders of his sobriety going up in smoke. These snapshots are all that he has left of his daughter. It'd been hard to let her go, even knowing that the man responsible was behind bars... what would he do now? "I'll think about it," he says.

"You'll do the right thing," Dispatch replies. "See you tomorrow."

There's a click and the line goes dead. Nick jumps to his feet and launches the phone at the television. Spiderweb-like fissures bloom from the impact crater. The pixels fail to communicate with each other, and the colors go all wrong. A large triangular swath of the screen goes lime green. The footage cuts to Benjie at a metal picnic table in the prisons exercise yard. He's looking wistfully out through the fence to the hills beyond. A yellow shard splits his sitting area in two. The sky is red with color distortion. Someone from behind the camera asks, "Do you think if Carmen were around today you'd still be friends?"

"Uh, oh yeah," Benjie says. "Even now."

The episode ends. The credits roll, and Nick passes out.

The next morning has Nick's head feeling like an egg about to hatch. He opens bloodshot eyes to find himself laying on the floor amidst his papers. He doesn't remember hauling the banker's boxes out. He kisses his finger and plants it on a photo of Carmen. *What am I going to do?* Bones creak as he pulls himself up to his feet. His saliva is thick and acrid tasting from last night's binge, so he lumbers over to the kitchen and puts his head under the faucet. Cool water runs across his face, soothing the pounding heat within his head. Then when the water clears of rust, he takes a mouthful, gargles and spits it back into the sink. He's drying himself with a hand towel when the phone goes off again. This time it's only his alarm: nine thirty. The television screen is still on — still fractured — and stuck on a pause menu.

It asks him: Are you still there?

He runs a hand over his shaved scalp. *Am I all here? Would I know if I wasn't?* He vaguely remembers talking to Dispatch on the phone but is unsure what had driven him to pick up in the middle of the night. Regardless, the pendejo Benjie is getting out today and Nick wants to be there... for better or worse.

Ponderosa's prison is surrounded by artificial hills made of red sand. These mounds make it so the entire complex sits in a gulley. Towers are situated at each corner of the high fence line and are made of grey concrete and tan brick. Local legend has it that an inmate tried to escape once. He allegedly managed to get through the fence but was shot through the head by an eagle-eyed sniper in the furthest tower. A camera crew is set up at the front gate, awaiting thirty-six-year-old Benjie to set foot outside the penitentiary for the first time in twenty years.

The road is surprisingly crowded for being so far outside the city limits. Nick parks his taxi on the shoulder across the street. A crowd of onlookers, fans of the series, watch and wait for Benjie along with the local news crew. Nick pulls a ball cap down low on his head and gets out of the vehicle in order to mingle with the crowd.

It isn't long before a lone figure in ill-fitting khakis and a faded jean jacket makes his way down the long-fenced corridor towards freedom. Prison food and weights had robbed Benjie of his girth and transformed him into a short lean man. Although the ruddy red cheeks remain. Nick shivers despite the asphalt radiating midday heat, baking him from below. The hairs on the back of his neck stand up. It's more like seeing a zombie than a ghost — a recognizable face and body, but devoid of the soul.

For years Nick had prepared to watch this man die, had dreamt of being there when the needle plunger was pushed. He tries to summon some of that rage, that kind that made him wish old sparky hadn't been outlawed. The kind of rage that makes eye for an eye seem reasonable. He finds that he can't. *Maybe Benjie is a victim of the docuseries as well.* Could the true villain be the corporation? Is it right to profit off the pain of grieving families? Parading corpses like science projects to pick apart; as if justice is no longer about right and wrong, but about who can argue their points best. Just how could they have eight one-hour-long episodes, interviewing every relation and suspect about how they knew Carmen, and not uncover who she was? How she would sing in the shower till there was no hot water left in the house or how she was such a fussy eater that she'd eat French fries but not a baked potato. *That her first word had been Dada.*

No one is here for Carmen, they are all here for Benjie. The crowd of onlookers rise from their lawn chairs and cheer. Some of the tailgaters shake up beer cans and open them, spraying foam everywhere. Women wave hand painted signs with hashtags like: **#WESTANDWITHBENJIE, #INNOCENTUNTILPROVENGUILTY, #MISSINGNECKLACE.** Benjie sees them too but quickly looks to the ground, his cheeks getting redder still. Then without looking up, he raises a fist into the air and the onlookers go wild. It sounds like the home team had just won the super bowl outside the prison.

A correctional officer stops Benjie at the gate. They exchange a few words, smile and shake hands. The guard opens the door and the inmate steps through a free man. More cheering. Someone lights off a few bottle rockets which go whistling overhead, their pops unheard amidst the jubilation. Microphones are held in front of Benjie's face.

"Benjie," says one reporter, "tell us how you feel?"

"Uh," Benjie scratches the stubble under his chin. "I guess I'm glad it's over."

"Benjie," another says, "what's the first thing you'll do now that you're out?"

"Oh I've been thinking about this one a lot," he answers. "I'm going to finally rent *Toy Story* from Blockbuster."

The reporters, crew and crowd all chuckle at this. No one is thinking of Carmen. Why should they? The public's hive mind has a short memory. They don't care much for the dead and gone. Benjie is alive; he might still have a future. Everyone likes a happy ending, don't they?

"Benjie, do you have anything to say to the family of Carmen Velasquez?"

After a pause, Benjie slowly replies, "You have no idea how sad I've been. Uh, thinking about how this series shows that, well, that the guy that killed Carmen is still out there. And well, that just makes it all fresh again, don't it? I understand how badly they wanted justice and uh, I just want them to know that I don't blame them for that."

No more than ten yards away, hidden amidst the throng of people, Nick clenches his jaw and nods absently as Benjie speaks. His old man had the same expression on his face when his mother passed. He hadn't understood it at the time, but he understands it now. It's the look of a strong man trying his best not to break. He wants to call out to Benjie to... to apologize. To fight. Let them have it out right there in front of the cameras. And after, maybe then Nick could cry. He opens his mouth once, twice, three times — but nothing comes out.

Shoulders slumping, he wants nothing more than to sit down or shower. He feels... dirty. He retires to the taxi cab and cranks the AC to max, content watching the rest from afar. Benjie shakes hands with his supporters, one of the tailgaters offers him a cold beer and he drinks it. His lips pucker at the taste and everyone laughs yet again. It strikes Nick just then that will have been Benjie's first legal drink. *Imagine, your first beer at thirty-six!*

When things begin to wind down, Nick flicks on the taxi's service light. Benjie shakes one last hand and clambers into the back seat. Nick starts the car and Benjie rattles off his grandmother's address. Benjie is flustered by all the activity. From the rearview mirror, Nick can make out the dopey half grin he's wearing. Nick starts the car and the locks click shut. With the hat and glasses Benjie hasn't recognized him.

"Gee," Benjie says after a few miles in silence, "I forgot how fast cars are. I remember, uh, that I used to get carsick. If I get carsick will you pull over?"

Benjie's knuckles are white on the armrests.

"Sure Benjie," Nick mumbles and his knuckles are white on the steering wheel.

"Say, uh, I didn't give you my name. Did you watch the series?"

"Something like that," Nick says, taking off the glasses.

Even so, it takes Benjie a minute to realize who is in the front seat. *Christ, have I aged that much or is the pendejo slower than I remember?*

"Mr.—Mr. Velasquez?" Benjie blinks rapidly. "What are you doing here?"

"You've been in for a long time Benjie, I work for the cab company now."

"I guess a lot has changed, huh?" Benjie sits back in his seat, relaxing ever so slightly.

"Everything has changed," Nick agrees, "and nothing. Carmen is still gone. Did you know, I got your parole denied? You were sixteen years old when Carmen was killed. You should have got parole after ten years. Does that piss you off?"

"I mean, yeah," Benjie says with a shrug. "But I had a long time to uh think, I mean while I was inside. At first, I felt like you were killing me, you know? Taking my best years, but then I thought — I thought you know, I'd probably do the same if our positions were reversed."

"Why did you do it Benjie?"

"I didn't Mr. Velasquez, I swear."

"I mean the docuseries?" Nick says.

"I'm innocent," Benjie says, "and it really helped that other fella, uh, a state over clear his name. It meant freedom. You don't know what it's like being called a murderer for twenty years when you and, uh, God know that you didn't do nothing."

"You know what it meant to me?" Nick says watching Benjie shake his head no in the rearview. "It meant that Carmen had to die all over again. Twenty years of people raising her from the dead, digging through the wreckage of my life; and for what? To help you? I was convinced you did it. Convinced that you took my sweet daughter away from me."

"And, uh what do you think now, uh, sir?"

"I don't even know anymore," Nick sighs. "Seems to me

that all these networks want to glorify murder and mystery, and in the end it don't matter if you did it or not. If you did kill Carmen they got their show, and if you didn't... well, they still got their show. Doesn't seem right to me and I'm just caught in the thresher."

The silence weighs heavy between them as they drive due south down the highway. The exit to Benjie's grandmother's house is a mile off. Tumbleweeds roll past in the opposite lane and get swept up in the swirls of dust left by the taxi cab as it blows past.

"You know," Benjie says, his face going red, "I loved her too. But I, uh, don't think she liked me that way you know?"

"Have you ever blacked out before, Benjie?"

"No," Benjie admits. "That was the first time. Could you uh, slow down Mr. Velasquez? I'm feeling ill."

The taxi goes past the exit, leaving Ponderosa behind.

Benjie's brow furrows. "Say, uh, where are we going?"

"We're going to Blockbuster buddy," Nick says. "I'm taking you to Blockbuster."

* * *

This story first appeared in the After Dinner Conversation—August 2021 issue.

Discussion Questions

1. If there was a Netflix-style docuseries about the person accused of killing your loved one, would you watch it?

2. Do you think that Nick will have peace now? If so, what is causing him to have that peace, and why didn't he have it sooner?

3. Does it matter to the story if Benjie was really innocent or guilty? Do your feelings about the story, or the decisions/changes in the characters change if Benjie secretly is the killer?

4. Is it fair that a Netflix investigation series helped prove Benjie's innocence and get him out of jail? Does it matter that there are other innocent people who weren't lucky enough to get their own Netflix special?

5. What would you have done (or said) if you had been Nick, driving the taxi, in the story?

* * *

Christmas In Ushuaia

Matias Travieso-Diaz

* * *

All people have had ill luck, but Jairus's daughter and Lazarus had the worst. Mark Twain

Laz pulled the parka closer to his body, ineffectually trying to ward off the gelid wind that blew from the mountains. Argentina was supposed to be warm in late December, but in Ushuaia, at the end of the world, the temperature rarely rose above fifty degrees. "Today, not even fifty," Laz mumbled. Talking to himself was just one of the habits that over the years had attached to him like fleas on a dog's fur.

He had not come to this remote outpost to see the sights—Ushuaia held little of interest to entice a seasoned traveler like himself; it was described in the tourist guides as merely "a sliver of steep streets and jumbled buildings below the snowcapped Martial Range" of the Andes. He was also not interested in a trip to Antarctica, or in hiking the steep trails of Andorra Valley or trekking to the Martial Glacier, a couple of hours from town. "I'm not athletic," he told himself; not that his arthritic knees would have allowed him to go ambling about as he used to in his youth.

He had signed up for a four-hour boat cruise on the Beagle Channel that would take him to his goal, the area around the Les Eclaireurs lighthouse. Sailing along the channel off Ushuaia, the boat had passed by sea lions basking on the rocks, cormorants sitting on nests, fur seals, and other wildlife he did not recognize. On Martillo Island, the boat had come close to what the guide described as one of the largest penguin colonies outside of Antarctica. Laz had taken numerous pictures, although he had no expectation he would ever show them to anyone.

The boat finally arrived at Les Eclaireurs lighthouse, an iconic symbol of Ushuaia that the locals called the "lighthouse at the end of the world." Its distinctive red and white stripes contrasted sharply with the backdrop of snow-capped mountains north of the channel. Laz would have liked to disembark, but this was not permitted.

The end point of the boat tour was small Bridges Island. Passengers got off and set out on a walk, in search of native flora and fauna. At one point along the trek, Laz paused to gaze at the sprawling view across the Beagle Channel, with Ushuaia in the distance and the lighthouse not far to the northeast.

An albatross, gliding on enormous wings, circled around Laz. It spiraled down and landed a few yards away, righted itself and began pecking at the ground with its longish hooked bill in search of morsels cast away by the sea. It paused for one moment, raised its head, and stared at Laz as if offering encouragement.

Laz extracted from his coat a small notebook with dirty,

worn covers and opened it.

Each page of the notebook bore line after line of minuscule, crabbed handwriting. Some of the entries had become blurred by contact with liquids; others were obliterated by thick horizontal lines. Some entries were in pencil, others in inks of various colors. There were gaps in some pages, as if the writer had given up on his task only to resume it sometime later.

Laz read aloud one of the entries on the first page, which stood out because it was a little larger than the others and seemed to be inscribed with greater force. He read: "They all laughed at seeing my legs encased in plaster casts. I said that I had to wear the casts for eight weeks to straighten my crooked leg bones, and they laughed even more." The rest of the entry had been blacked out.

Laz tore the page and flung it away, and the strong breeze carried it towards the icy realms to the south. At the sound of ripping paper, the albatross jumped a little, but planted again its long, webbed feet on the rocky soil and resumed its dinner.

Laz started to read aloud again from his diary, but had to stop almost at once: the fierce wind choked him and paralyzed his throat. He continued tearing page after page from the notebook, sometimes stopping to read to himself a few lines, tears forming in the corners of his eyes at some remembered event. The wind carried away briskly each of the pages; the albatross paid no attention to the ceremony after the disturbance caused by the first sheet.

A voice near Laz's ears broke his concentration: "What are you doing?" It was the guide, bringing the rest of the passengers back to the boat. "Littering is a criminal offense in Tierra del Fuego. Stop it or I will have to report you."

Laz smiled sheepishly. "Sorry. I'm done." He pocketed the remains of the notebook and joined the caravan.

His bare hotel room weighed heavily on Laz's spirit. He had to get out, find some company. There was light in the sky even though it was past nine thirty p.m. He went into the first restaurant he came across and asked the girl at the reception booth: "Are you still serving dinner?"

"Of course," she replied. Her Spanish had a strange undertone, as if it was not her native tongue. "Yesterday was the solstice. We will be open until midnight every day, including Christmas, through the end of the month. Would you like to be seated?"

Laz nodded and was led into a room with large rustic tables and high back, dark wooden chairs. There were simple Christmas decorations on the walls, wreaths of plastic holly and Santas and reindeer imported from northern countries.

The restaurant was packed; however, around the corner they had an overflow section that was almost full already. There were no single tables available, so the hostess indicated that Laz would have to share space with four other diners. Under normal circumstances, Laz would have walked away. But that night he welcomed being with others; besides, this was high season in Ushuaia and other restaurants might be just as crowded. He sat down and greeted his companions.

The table was occupied by a tourist couple that spoke in some European language Laz did not recognize; they ignored everybody and spent the rest of their stay talking loudly among themselves. The other couple were locals: a dark, middle-aged man and his ample, fair-skinned wife. Laz sat next to the wife, who announced: "I'm María Eugenia, and this is my husband

Héctor." "My name is Lázaro Cruz," Laz replied. María Eugenia immediately drew Laz into an amiable, mostly one-sided conversation.

As a waiter brought him a menu, Laz noticed that the European couple had their entrees—a lamb dish and some stew—before them; the locals were starting on their appetizers. Half a dozen beer bottles littered the surface of the table.

"What are you guys having?" asked Laz to María Eugenia.

"We are sharing the king crab appetizer, which is the specialty of the house," she beamed.

"Is it good?" inquired Laz politely.

"Here, taste it." María Eugenia speared a morsel on her fork and handed it to Laz. He was somewhat startled by the unhygienic gesture, but blinked nervously and accepted the gift. "This is very good," he acknowledged.

"What else is good around here?" he then asked, emboldened by the woman's familiarity.

"Just about everything," replied María Eugenia, chewing on her crab. "I am partial to the black hake, which they cook in parchment. And you must drink the local beer." She pointed to one of the empty bottles on the table. "That's Cape Horn Stout, my favorite."

The waiter returned and Laz was ready to order. "I'll have the king crab appetizer and the black hake for the main course. And a bottle of Cape Horn Stout, please."

The beer came first. It was dark, sweet and slightly bitter. By the time the appetizer came, Laz was on his second bottle.

The food was quite good, and the beer grew on Laz as he ordered yet another bottle. He was only a casual drinker, and by the time he finished with the hake he was on his fourth bottle and already feeling tipsy.

His chitchat with María Eugenia had continued unabated through dinner. As the waiter brought out the dessert menu, the lady bent her head in his direction and asked him in a confidential tone: "So, since you are not on your way to Antarctica, what brought you out to the end of the world?"

Laz was feeling pretty drunk by that time, and whispered back: "I... came to rid myself of my sorrows." He hiccupped.

"What do you mean?" replied María Eugenia, surprised.

"It's a long story," slurred Laz. "What should I get for dessert?"

Amid bites of tiramisu and sips of disappointingly weak coffee, Laz told a tale from his childhood. "I was raised in a middle-class household in Buenos Aires. After the birth of my sister Elisa, my mother was too weak to handle the household chores by herself, so she contacted the rector of a Salesian Brothers congregation in our neighborhood, to see if they could provide an orphan girl that could be hired to help around our house. There were no children available, but they had a recent female arrival from Tierra del Fuego: Kuluána, a Yaghan Indian of indeterminate age who had been rescued from her declining village by Salesian missionaries. The mission had closed down for some reason and the wards they were trying to civilize were scattered all over Argentina.

"Kuluána was old and nurturing, and became a second mother to Elisa and me. I would confide to her many of my childhood pains and fears, not daring to raise them with my distracted mother or my very distant father. Once, when I was thirteen or fourteen, Kuluána spotted me hiding in one corner, crying. She came over and, putting her arm around my heaving shoulders, asked: 'Lazarito, what's the matter? Why are you crying?'

"Between sobs, I related what I felt was a world-ending tragedy: 'Elena Santos has dumped me. She says I'm too boring, and would rather be friends with Arturo.' She gave a short laugh and replied: 'And what do you propose to do about it?'

"'I dunno,' I answered, and broke into loud sobs. 'I want to die!' Kuluána assumed a vague expression, as if trying to bring back something from the dim past. Finally, she squeezed my shoulder and said: 'Lazarito, where I come from, a village way south of here, we have an ancient custom. Whenever we feel overwhelmed by sorrow, we get on a canoe and paddle down, get close to the big frozen water, and cry aloud the name of the person or thing that's hurting us, so that the wind will carry it away to the gods at the land of eternal night and we will be rid of it. I never tried doing this myself, but my kippa, my mother, said that it had worked for her and others in the village.'

"'Do I need to travel all the way south before I can feel better?' I rebelled.

"'No, child,' she answered. 'The pain will soon go away by itself; you'll see.'

"I didn't believe Kuluána but the pain slowly faded away, as she had predicted. All the same, I started keeping a diary in which I would record all the sad events of my life in the off chance I might have to call them out some day. With the years, my sorrows multiplied and my diary became full, little by little. Last month my lifetime companion 'passed way' leaving me totally alone and feeling as disconsolate as I was the day of my conversation with Kuluána. Remembering the Yaghan folk story, I decided to take a special Christmas vacation in Ushuaia and scream my woes into the land of eternal night. I went on a cruise of the Beagle Channel with the intention of shouting out each of the sorrows and misfortunes of my life. Only it was too damned cold, so instead of talking I just tore away the pages of my diary and cast them out to the wind. I'm sure the gods of the eternal night know how to read."

Héctor, who had remained silent through the dinner, lay his beer bottle on the table and asked: "What sort of stuff did you have in the notebook? Just the bad things?"

Laz, who was near passing out, revived enough to reply: "No, all sorts of things. As the girl said years ago, I'm boring. I write everything down, sometimes in detail."

"And you tossed the whole thing out to the gods?"

The question startled Laz and woke him up a little.

"Yeah, but they are supposed to read only the bad parts."

María Eugenia picked up from her husband. "And how are they supposed to know which parts are good and which bad?"

Laz was saved from having to answer the question by the European couple, who had just paid their check and got up with a clattering of chairs, said *"buenas noches"* in barbarous Spanish, and taken off.

Laz was still watching the Europeans make their exit when María Eugenia resumed: "See, it's not always easy to tell. Our son Carlos died in an avalanche earlier this year. We were, and still are, devastated by the loss. He was our only child, and we miss him terribly." She was for a moment overcome with emotion, but she checked herself and resumed: "But his death has brought my husband and I closer together, and we are enjoying helping raise little María Luisa, our granddaughter."

Héctor cut in: "When I was a young man, I was fired from a job as insurance adjustor because my manager wanted to make room for his nephew to be brought in, fresh out of high school. I was appalled and downcast by the injustice, but in the process of looking for another job I met María Eugenia. So, you can say that a great ill led to happiness after the fact. Didn't something like that ever happen to you?"

Laz started to protest. "Well, that may have occurred in an instance or two, but there is no comparison between getting fired from a job and losing your wife or your parents, and experiencing other losses, as I have."

María Eugenia would not let him go on. "Yes, if you live long enough, you'll gather your share of sadness. But if you try to erase everything in your past, your life will become as empty as your notebook after you had cast its pages to the wind."

"Maybe the gods of the eternal night don't know how to read, after all," replied Laz vacantly, resting his head on the table and starting to snore.

María Eugenia elbowed him back to wakefulness. "Time to go to bed, my friend. Tomorrow is Christmas. Would you like to come have a holiday dinner with us?"

"That would be nice," replied Laz, slowly getting to his arthritic feet. "Let's go get the checks."

Laz insisted on picking up the tab for his newly acquired friends. "That's unnecessary," protested María Eugenia. Laz shushed her aside. "I owe you a debt of gratitude, for you guys have made me think. I'm not sure, but perhaps this is a good time for me to take stock and appreciate the miracle that it is just to be alive, no matter the ups and downs." He struggled to get his parka on, and on his way back to the hotel a thought occurred to him: "I bet I could reproduce from memory much of what was in that notebook. I might give it a try."

* * *

This story first appeared in the After Dinner Conversation—June 2021 issue.

Discussion Questions

1. María Eugenia says, "And how are they supposed to know which parts are good and which bad?" How do you?
2. Is the "bad things can turn out to be good in the future" thing just a coping mechanism humans use to soften the blow of bad experiences?
3. María Eugenia says, "But if you try to erase everything in your past, your life will become as empty as your notebook after you had cast its pages to the wind." Are there aspects of our past that can be safely erased without making our lives more empty?
4. If you could erase any of your negative experiences, would you? If so, which one(s) and why?
5. Which is the better reason not to erase memories, "the greatness of life in its diversity of positive and negative experiences" or "the greatness of life is in the positive experiences, which may only come from negative experiences?" What is the difference in these two statements regarding a life outlook?

* * *

All My Tomorrows

J. Grace Pennington

* * *

It was Misha's first day minding the shop, and already she'd broken the fifth rule. Always lock the door immediately. When you had the most valuable merchandise in the universe, you had to take the utmost precautions.

She hadn't meant to disobey. It was just that when she had walked in, she forgot everything and stood for a full five minutes just inside the door, feeling the lights and colors reflected in the expression she felt on her face. She knew it by heart, but never had it been <u>hers</u>, to care for and manage and watch over.

A jolt shook the entire shop, causing her to stumble and clutch at one of the file cabinets for support. It seemed to jolt her memory as well, and she jumped as though she'd been slapped, and double bolted the rusty metal door shut.

The rumble subsided, and quiet settled upon the shop again. Turning back around, she saw that the drawer she'd gripped to stay upright had come open slightly, and she pushed it closed and latched it. It was one of the older drawers, and the latch was brown and gritty feeling, and when she pulled her hand away, there was a film of orange rust on her fingers. She started to wipe it down the front of her dress, then stopped herself and just rubbed her fingers together to brush it off.

"That one must be almost gone," she murmured, and then listened to the very faint echo of her words. She'd never been alone here before. Turning her head, she surveyed the long rows and columns of drawers, reaching far into the darkness, everywhere except where the thick aluminum silicate glass window spanned several feet of one wall, looking out into space. Drawers everywhere, each barely bigger than her hand, reaching so far and so high that she had no hope of ever seeing the end of them. Some of the cabinets were so rusty they were crumbling, and some were still the dull but polished maroon that was standard for the GCC. On each drawer was a name, burned into it by the computer system, and the words "Galactic Cabinet Company" with a phone number. Her gaze followed the sturdy black cables that connected every single drawer to the processor far above her on the ceiling. She couldn't see where they were plugged in, it was so high up that the darkness hid it, but tiny lights from the computer sparkled like stars.

Once as a child, she'd tried to describe the shop to a friend, and the friend had commented, "It sounds terribly dull." Then, she knew she'd never try to describe it again.

No matter how tight the GCC made the cabinets, they couldn't keep the colors, the light, the darkness, the smells, the temperatures, the tastes, the emotions, and the sounds from escaping through the cracks. There was no greater thrill than walking by a drawer and feeling a sliver of anger escape, along with a slight scent of roast beef and a dash of warmth.

Sometimes she'd catch a snippet of wonder and beauty, tinted with purple and flavored with mint. Other times, a shiver would shake her, and she'd find that she was cold, and would look to see a dark mist seeping from one of the drawers, along with a stench that tasted somehow hollow. Better yet was when a sudden burst of every color would flow freely and sparkle up to the ceiling, accompanied with every feeling that existed all rolled into one. Those moments were always Misha's favorites, because they were so beautiful. Then her father had explained that that meant someone was dying, and it made her sad, too, but still happy, because it was the best thing in the universe.

And then it would be time to replace that drawer. New people were always being born, and an old rusty drawer would be shipped out, and a new maroon one would come in, ready to be burned with a new name, and filled with new files. Except sometimes, a maroon drawer would go out, and that made Misha sad, because somewhere, somehow, someone had lost their child.

Slowly, she unwound her scarf, keeping her eyes on the cabinets. Wisps of color escaped and floated up to the ceiling, and she caught sight of a hint of green. Tossing scarf and cap on the floor behind her, she darted forward. Green was her favorite. Green was fresh and clean and open and rested, and it usually meant peace. Dodging the other colors, she reached it just in time to let it brush the tips of her fingers. She grinned. This one was a childhood memory, she knew it was. She smelled wet grass, and felt a burst of contentment.

She sighed as it floated away. That was a good one to have caught. She was glad for whoever was remembering it right now. Her father had told her that when bits showed, it was because someone was remembering. Looking at the name on the drawer, she read "John Fillmore Tucker III." It was still red, with only patches here and there that were just showing rust. John Fillmore Tucker III was a middle-aged man, by the look of it.

She touched the latch, and it slipped out easily. Driven by curiosity, she pulled the drawer open with one finger, just a crack. Green spilled out into the air, and she felt a full blast of the day. It was dew, and a shirt not buttoned straight, and sharp, crisp, open air, and not thinking about anything, and all the smells and sounds of morning. She was there, she could see the overcast sun and feel the childlike dreams and plans and lack of fear.

Closing her eyes, she slammed the drawer shut and replaced the latch. The click echoed in the room, and she felt shame burn her cheeks. Rule number four broken. You weren't supposed to open the drawers unless there was a technical difficulty. Otherwise, the computer handled all the files itself.

She scurried to the window and settled herself into the swivel chair at the terminal. The terminal, because even though there were others they were rusted over and no longer functioned. Only one had been kept working, because these days only one was needed. In the old days, the shop had been kept busy from morning until night, but now it had been relegated to the stuff of legend, until only a determined few ever came to the out-of-the-way asteroid asking for an exchange of days. Misha remembered when there had been two terminals open, and her father and grandfather would work them, but she had been only seven then. Now things were quiet, Father was getting older, and all her brothers and sisters were grown and had left the asteroid and the shop. Things were so quiet that

Father deemed an only-just-sixteen-year-old girl qualified to run the shop now, while he helped her brother move to a planet.

Leaning back in the chair, she looked out the clouded glass at the stars and other asteroids. A piece of rock hurtled toward her and struck at the base of the shop, causing another jolt to rifle through the asteroid. She clutched the arms of the chair to steady herself, feeling the cracked leather pinch her fingers, until the quivers passed.

It wasn't nearly as interesting over by the terminals. There was nothing to look at except space, and glass, and cobwebs, and the old, brittle copies of the manual for the computer system. She didn't dare touch the books, for fear they would crumble at a single nudge. And there were no smells except rust and musky leather, and there were no sounds except when a rock hit, or the creaking of the chair if she moved even a centimeter. And there was rarely any emotion to experience except boredom.

She had no way of knowing how much time passed as she sat there. The system would shut itself down when work hours were over, and then she would go home. Until then, she was just to sit there in her best dress and wait, maybe for nothing. She peered back over her shoulder at the colors escaping from the drawers. No one was coming. She'd heard her father say that they only had customers once a week these days, sometimes less. What would it hurt to explore, just a little?

The shop shook again, and she gripped the arms, waiting for the world to stop shaking. But this time, it didn't keep on trembling. It gave a tiny heave, then paused, then seemed to rest. She knew that feeling, and she felt another grin shape her lips as she turned to the window, straightened her collar, leaned her elbows on the desk, and looked as professional as sixteen can.

At the end of the long dock that stretched out before her was a speeder. It wasn't one of the rusty old buckets that usually stopped there, it was—the only word that flashed into her head was <u>fiery</u>. It was yellow, with streaks of red licking toward the shiny cockpit. She sat up even straighter and watched, trying to keep her mouth set in a firm, business-like line.

The door of the speeder opened upwards, and a man stepped out. It was too far away for her to tell more than his gender and the color of his clothes, which were also red and yellow. He closed the door, pushing it closed instead of slamming it. Then he straightened up, and walked up the long dock and toward the shop.

Misha's mouth kept threatening to grin, and she pinched the back of her hand to force herself to remain serious as he approached her terminal, every step measured and firm. Her first customer! A real customer, coming to buy a day from <u>her</u>!

As he came to the glass, he reached out and polished a bit of it with the back of his sleeve. She watched as the thin layer of dust peeled away to reveal his features one by one, the brown hair falling over his forehead, the handsome, middle-aged face, the tired, blue eyes. The eyes looked right at her as he tapped on the window with his knuckles, and she gave a polite smile, and spoke into the intercom.

"Hello, and welcome to the Shop of Yesterdays. How may I help you?"

For a moment he just looked at her, his listless eyes seeming to bore through her and ask her a question that she did not understand. His clothes seemed much too young for him, she noted then, as if he were playing dress-up as a twenty-five-year-old when he was really forty. And his eyes looked more than tired, but she didn't understand it. It was something she'd felt sometimes, from the drawers, but she didn't know the word for it, and she had an impression somehow that it was a word she wasn't old enough to know.

"It's real then," he said.

"The shop? Yes sir, quite real indeed."

He rolled up his sleeve, and she flipped the identification switch in front of her.

"Press your wrist to the red light so the system can read you, please," she instructed, and he obeyed, laying the front of his wrist against the light that blinked on the glass. Old tattoos traced up his forearm and into his sleeve, and she wondered how far they went, and then felt her cheeks grow pink. She looked away.

The red light flashed twice, then vanished, and the computer whirred as it identified him. It only took three seconds for the name to flash on the desk before her, "John Fillmore Tucker III."

She jerked her head up to his face, allowing her surprise to show for a moment. Then she looked over her shoulder at the drawers. The one she'd looked into earlier was illuminated with the white light of the computer.

She looked at him again, lost in her own thoughts for a moment. This wasn't the kind of man she'd imagined. Somehow what was in his eyes didn't match the morning she'd felt in his files. Then she blushed yet again. You were never supposed to go silent when dealing with a customer. You were just supposed to serve them efficiently.

"What can I get you today, sir?" she asked into the

intercom.

Again, he was silent for a moment, and when he spoke, she felt surprised by the fact that he had. "How much does one yesterday cost?"

This she also knew by heart. "One year, sir."

His expression didn't change. She was used to eyebrows raising. It did seem a steep price, three hundred and sixty-five tomorrows for a single yesterday. But that was only if you didn't understand how priceless yesterdays were. They weren't like a can of beans or a new pair of trousers. A yesterday was time, and memory, and life, and senses, and heart, and knowledge, and ideas all rolled up into one. They were expensive to catalog and keep and transfer, and Misha's family were the only ones in the entire universe who knew how.

But he didn't widen his eyes, or even move a facial muscle. He only said, "I see. I only have two hundred."

Without another word, but still looking her straight in the eyes, he rolled down his sleeve. Then he turned around and took a step.

She remembered the dew, and the green, and the fresh smell of morning, and called out, "Sir?"

He turned around, looking exactly the same as he had before.

Don't engage the customers in personal conversation. Rule three.

"I... I'm curious." She stammered. It wasn't professional to stammer. "What is important about this day?"

He stepped back toward the window again, and studied her face for a moment. Then he said, "You're too young to understand."

"Try me."

A beat of silence drove the nervousness further into her, and then he relaxed his posture, and allowed one corner of his lips to turn up softly. "It was the last good day."

"Why?"

"Because the day after that, I learned something I wasn't ready for."

Misha recalled the empty child mind, and how relaxed and trusting it had felt when she'd sensed it for a moment. "What happened?"

"Learning wasn't enough. I went looking for more, and nobody knew about it except me."

"Did you find it?"

"Yes. But then, looking once wasn't enough." He stopped, closing his mouth firmly as if to keep any more from escaping. But when she prompted "What then?" he continued.

"Then, I met the woman I wanted to spend my life with. I didn't tell her about the things, thinking they would go away, when I had her to fill me. For a while they did. But then they returned, and I couldn't hide from her forever."

As he spoke, Misha glanced down at his left hand, and detected a band of slightly paler skin around the base of the third finger.

"She told me to leave, so I got on my ship and never came back."

She looked back at his face. It was a strong, right face, except for the dull eyes... "Why do you only have two hundred left?"

This time he hesitated. He focused behind her, at the drawers, expression not changing, and then ran the tip of his tongue between his lips and took a breath. "It dragged me further down, and moved from my mind into my body, until I'd lost count of the people who had shared it, and it drove me further and further into the pit until it claimed my health. And that, child, is why I have only two hundred tomorrows, and it is also why I'd trade every last one of them for a single day of how things used to be."

Misha knew that he didn't expect her to understand, but she'd been around every yesterday in the universe too long not to grasp what the loss of innocence and the spiral into darkness felt like.

Rule number two was never to negotiate price with customers.

"I'll take two hundred."

"You don't even know what day it is..." he protested. As if any day could be worth such a small price.

"I think I do."

She reached forward and pressed the transaction button, and a message flashed in red on the desk. "Error. Insufficient tomorrows remaining."

Rule number one was to never override the system.

Without so much as a shudder, she pressed the override button, stood up, and turned toward the only illuminated drawer in the room. It was oozing green now, refracting off the air like light through the surface of the water. She unlatched it, opened it, and closed her eyes for a moment as the freshly cut grass and the pure contentment flooded into her. Then she opened her eyes just a crack.

The array of colors felt as though it would blind her, and the incense of darkness, despair, hope, falling, flying, pleasure, pain, guilt, and loss slapped her. She was afraid, she felt dirty, everything was confusion and needing to find someone to share her, and feeling empty and dark. Forcing herself to weather the storm, she scanned the files for the brightest and last spot of green in the horde of days, and reached in to grasp it. It burned her hand, and she screamed, then she managed to yank it out, and slam the drawer shut before collapsing to her knees, panting.

She breathed as her head cleared, hardly feeling the spot of light in her clenched fist. She was herself. Misha. She was home, she was in the shop. She was only-just-sixteen, she loved colors, she was young, she was happy, and she was safe.

The buzzing in her ears cleared, and she heard a faint pounding nearby. Over and over. Then a voice, a man's voice. "Little girl! Little girl, are you alright?"

She stood up, her legs wobbling like the preserves that Mother made. The day burned in her hand, but it didn't hurt anymore. Looking down, she saw that green was shining between her tightly clenched fingers.

The man stopped pounding his fists on the glass as she stood, and wobbled toward him. Still keeping her hand closed, she eased into her chair, still panting. "I'm fine," she answered, realizing only then that she hadn't responded to his question. She managed a smile. "I have what you wanted."

She took another deep breath, and this one finally filled her lungs, making her feel strong again. "Put your right forefinger in the hole, please."

He stuck the indicated finger into the tiny gray hole in the glass. She brought her fist close to the capsule on her side, and uncurled her fingers to reveal the day, a small, green particle, in the center of her palm. She picked it up with her other hand, and slipped it securely into the capsule, glad she'd watched her grandfather do manual transfers many years before.

Taking another deep breath, she pressed the send button, and watched his face wince as the day pricked into the tip of his finger. "It will activate at midnight, and last twenty-four hours," she said, forcing her voice to be steady. "I hope it's all you wanted."

Those eyes bored into hers again, but all he said was, "It will be."

"Goodbye."

He turned without another word, and strode back toward his speeder. He pulled open the door, slipped in, and flew off, giving the asteroid another jerk as he disconnected.

Misha watched as he disappeared into the stars. The shop was silent again. The colors went on dancing out of the drawers, and she sat in her chair until the lights flickered off. She got up, felt her way to her scarf and cap, and put them both on. Then she unlocked the door, opened it, and gave the shop one last look.

Then she closed the door and locked it.

* * *

This story first appeared in the After Dinner Conversation—July 2020 issue.

Discussion Questions

1. In the story, the exchange is one year to get to relive one day. Is that a fair price? What price, if any, would you pay to get to re-experience a day?

2. What would be the benefits or detriments to a person by being able to relive a day (*good or bad*) in their past? Does your opinion change if you were able to make different choices (*that didn't affect the present*) rather than simply watch the day unfold?

3. Is it a cruelness or a kindness to have a service that allows someone to relieve a past day?

4. What would be your criteria for judging the day you would want to re-experience? Would it be a special occasion, a particularly happy day, a "first" [blank] day, a sad day, a day you made a critical mistake, or something else? What day (*if any*) would you like to re-experience and why?

5. By trading a year for a day, aren't you assuming that none of the 365 days you are trading in will live up to the day you are trading it for? Is that fair to those future days? Or those future people that you would have experienced the day with?

* * *

The Momentary Paradise

Olga Pavlinova Olenich

* * *

She'd seen a Japanese film in which the newly dead faced a panel of long-dead bureaucrats and were asked, on the spot, to choose the moment in their lives in which they would live eternally, suspended in the feeling and the physicality of the chosen moment. This meant that—provided you had lived a good life, whatever that might mean—you could dictate the terms of your own paradise within the limitations of your previous mortal experience.

She was sure that the idea for the film was not a new one because she knew that there were no new ideas, especially in films where everything was borrowed and reconstructed and presented with various degrees of verisimilitude. In the case of the Japanese film—or what parts of it she'd seen because it was screened on television in the early hours of a Sunday morning while she drifted in and out of sleep—the level of verisimilitude was very high though she had to admit that her state of drifting may have given it more of a feeling of truth than was actually there. Or perhaps her semi-conscious state took away any of the criteria of verisimilitude and gave the film the reality of dreams, given that there was such a reality. However, she was not going to begin yet another argument with herself on the nature of dreams and reality. She was, nevertheless, struck with the idea behind the film and began to trawl the ocean of her own experiences for the one moment she would have liked to be suspended in forever. Her formaldehyde moment. Her destiny.

She thought she had lived a good life, so far. Goodish. Relatively so. Of course, she was no saint though the saints she had investigated—and she had, at some stage, been very interested in the lives of saints—generally had some colorful experiences before the patina of sainthood and time had covered them up and made them less glaringly at odds with the general expectations people have of their saints.

Her choices swung wildly from day to day, depending on how the particular day had gone. If it had been a day at home, in the peace of her garden with her son rattling around inside the house, she unhesitatingly chose that moment when she had first seen her newborn child. A defining moment. The great icon Mother.

But if the happy rattling around in the house changed to that string of small demands or that litany of little protests that are the stuff of day-to-day motherhood, she would judge that the moment, for all of its romance, was not all it was cracked up to be. It was, as it were, uninformed and in that it was poorer.

How could she choose not to know her child? And if she had chosen a moment other than the birth, then that's what she would have chosen: forever, never to know her child. She would have chosen a moment about herself. She would have chosen a moment excluding her child.

If it had been one of those days when she wanted to run away, she chose from those sorts of moments on top of a mountain or on a cliff or watching the sun set behind a line of hills or watching it rise over the ocean.

Moments of poetry. Transporting moments, rising above and beyond all other moments in some spiritual sense. The trouble, of course, was choosing the particular moment to the exclusion of other such soaring moments. Should she exclude the roar of the waves on the Great Ocean Road, should she let go of Venice at daybreak, should she sacrifice the stars and the sea and the temple at Mahabalipuram, should her moment on the ramparts of Novgorod the Great be forever lost to her for that moment on the deck of a ship when the wave rose in front of her like a wall of jade? It was hard, choosing the moment. It was harder, perhaps, than the choice an artist makes when he decides to suspend a moment between the sides of his canvas. She wondered, for instance, how Leonardo had chosen the moment at which to capture the Annunciation. Did he see the angel in flight before he settled it on the carpet of flowers, its wings still parallel, its hand raised in perfect line with the table on which the Madonna's own delicate hand rested? Was the symmetry of the moment or of Leonardo's making? Perhaps it was of both. What guarantee was there that the moment she might choose was not one she had reconstructed in her memory to be more beautiful, more harmonious, more like Leonardo's masterpiece than it had actually been? Could her own aesthetic sense conspire with the impatient panel to push her into a false choice?

After a week of deliberation and uncertainty, she awoke to see that the Japanese film had taken hold of her in a way that was uncharacteristically irrational, and she wondered if she was on the brink of madness. She mustered her thoughts into some sort of disciplined order and decided that her dreamlike state had seeped too deeply into her imagination. It was a rational decision to look at the film again in the sober light of day. She searched the weekly television guide to find the name of the film but found that the advertised program for the timeslot was bafflingly labeled *Religious Program,* as if the person compiling the guide had given up putting names to things. She could see the point. Actually, given the nature of the film, or at least the nature of it as she had interpreted it, the label was not too far off the mark.

She rang a few friends and put out an email at work to no avail. Nobody had heard of the film and, furthermore, nobody who had been awake at that time of night had been interested in watching television, let alone in wasting time on a *Religious Program.* She guessed their lives were a bit more interesting than hers at the moment. Perhaps the film did not exist; perhaps the idea was her own. But she knew this was impossible because she knew there were no new ideas, so she went back to choosing her moment because she felt that it was only when she was secure in her choice that the film and its insidious idea would finally lose their hold. She went to her old diaries for clues, but the clues were hidden in the jumble of self-indulgent words, words that embarrassed her, words that made her think that most of her life was made of such trivia that the glorious moment, wherever it was, was so drowned in accumulated rubbish that it could never be retrieved.

And yet she continued to think about it, turning over her life again and again in search of the paradise moment. One day she was sitting on the veranda watching a blackbird sitting in a tree. It crossed her mind that paradise might be as simple as this: her sitting on the veranda, the bird sitting in the tree. But it was somehow too pat, this simplicity. The end of an American film perhaps, but not the answer to the Japanese one.

Actually, the answer was all too obvious. And she found it just in time to retrieve the normal patterns of her life. The film was just a film. The idea was just an idea, and the glorious moment was only glorious because it was preceded by other moments and followed by still more moments and washed over by longer periods of time until it became colored and clouded and only sometimes illuminated by flashes of memory. What was being offered up by the long-dead bureaucrats in the film was not a paradise but a hell, and that, in the nature of things, no person had ever lived, would ever live the kind of good life required to deserve eternal residency in paradise. So it made sense that the bureaucrats, the gatekeepers, could only offer up a paradise in keeping with the limitations of the candidates who, like herself, were so taken up with themselves that they believed in their own moments and actually thought that their experiences—no, that *one* of their experiences, no, that a single *moment* in that experience—could be blown up into a full-scale heaven.

The phone rang. Reluctantly she left the veranda and the blackbird. It was her colleague, the film buff who had taken up the challenge of identifying the film with a vengeance. He was a Kurosawa expert, or so he said, so the fact that the film was

Japanese made it a matter of honor for him. She could tell immediately from the tone of his voice that honor had been satisfied. "The film," he said triumphantly, "is called *After Life*."

She was struck by the predictability of the title. Of course, the filmmakers would have had to call it something like that because, while they had appropriated the idea, they had no actual idea of its meaning. The proposition, surely, was that there was no After Life. There was only a Past Life, specifically there was one moment in a past life stretched from *here*, wherever that was, to *after*, which had no points of reference except for the past. She felt strongly that the word *after* had no place in the title of the film. She said so and she gave her reasons in a synoptic form because she wanted to get back to the veranda. "I think you have misinterpreted *After Life*," he said condescendingly. She laughed. She said it was a common problem, this misinterpretation of the afterlife. He didn't get it. She hung the phone up and went back to the veranda where the blackbird had chosen its moment to sweep down and take a hunk out of her croissant. Inside, the child was awake, rattling around in his room, looking for his shoes.

* * *

This story first appeared in the After Dinner Conversation—February 2023 issue.

Discussion Questions

1. If, like the story, you could dictate the terms of your own paradise within the limitations of your previous mortal experience, what moment in time would pick to live in for eternity?

2. What criteria did you use for picking your heavenly moment from your own life? Was it based on a moment of wonder, a moment of triumph, a moment of peace, or something else?

3. The narrator worries that by picking one moment, she is excluding all other moments. Does knowing this change your decision? What moments would you be most disappointed in having to leave behind and why?

4. What is the essence of heaven for you? Could it be, as the narrator suggests, a simple moment of "sitting on the veranda, the bird sitting in the tree"?

5. If you had the chance to opt into the version of paradise in this story for eternity, or cease to exist after your death, which would you choose, and why?

* * *

The Causes of The First World War

Paul Brownsey

* * *

Dear Jamie,

I hope you are well. I am not. I think I shan't live long. I have cirrhosis and peripheral neuritis and other things. Crichton Lodge is quite a pleasant place. My brother helps with the fees at present. I would like to see you again. I think about the past a lot. We went swimming together and to a party at Killearn. We went to see Torch Song Trilogy. They were good times.

All the best,
Fred Archibald

* * *

It was just as well that when the letter arrived, Alex was away, researching his book in the Foreign Office archives, because he has this odd idea that any contact with people either of us was involved with before we met is something like retrospective infidelity. I'd not seen that handwriting for over thirty years, but I recognized it on the envelope at once, even though it was more wavery now.

It must have taken a lot for Fred to write that letter. In the old days it was impossible to extract from him any expression of wanting to see me. If I suggested a drink or a film, he'd go silent and then say, "Okay," like someone reluctantly fitting an additional obligation into a heavy schedule. Which he did not have, because early on I checked out his address. The sight of his name—only his—on the door of what seemed to be a very small flat somehow confirmed our developing intimacy. From a distance I watched him enter the close, getting home from his work, and he didn't come out again all evening.

Poor Fred. Even his name was a nothing name. Others might have announced themselves as "Freddie," which reaches out in a friendly way, or "Frederick," which stands on dignity, but it was as if he didn't care how others saw him, and "Fred" would do if it was necessary to refer to him. The things he mentioned from our past were the more poignant because he wouldn't be dying in a care home where he couldn't afford the fees, if I hadn't treated him so shittily.

* * *

"We went swimming."

He remembered how we met. On my Wednesday evenings at the pool, I noticed this tall, gangly, black-bearded guy. Too few muscles to suggest he wanted a gym body—a good sign. Ordinary navy-blue swimming shorts. He didn't remove them to shower and always changed in a closed cubicle. He didn't interact with others at the pool—less like someone deliberately avoiding interaction, more as if it didn't occur to him that interaction was possible. I had an inkling as to what lay inside this shell, and I set out to crack it. After four or five weeks, I risked, "Hello." He stared at me for a long-puzzled moment before saying "Hello" back—not, you'd have thought, because he recognized me, but because politeness surfaced and told him that was how you replied.

We had similar black sports bags, and one week I deliberately put mine next to his. I was overjoyed when he accidentally picked up the wrong one, allowing me to chatter away about the bags' similarity and how the pool and changing rooms were well maintained, weren't they, and how he was a regular, wasn't he? My heartiness sounded horribly false against his minimal replies—"Yes," after a bit of thinking—but I wasn't going to lose the opportunity to say, "Maybe we could go for an after-swim drink sometime," saying it as a farewell as I waved and hurried off, because I sensed it would be no good to press the matter further just then.

I let it lie for a few weeks, just contenting myself with an offhand "hi" and getting a delayed echo back. When at last I said, "So what about that drink?" my voice implied it had already been settled we'd go for a drink sometime.

"Okay."

"So, when?"

"Now?" Like someone guilty at having forgotten something he'd promised to do.

I took him to Tennent's Bar. Between the drinks we bought each other, he ordered extra whiskies for himself, but only like someone who just happened to take more toast at breakfast than most people.

I told him that prior to being stormed by a posse of feminists in the 1970s, Tennent's had been a male-only bar. "There was even a gay corner," I slipped in. His eyes, normally rather blank, seemed suddenly to pulse—with interest?—with alarm?—with both? After a silence he asked, like someone inviting a confession of something very personal, if I went hillwalking. I wondered if isolation on a wild, remote hillside would bring on the moment when we fell into each other's arms, so I said, "Let's fix a date for a walk."

Apparently, though, solitary hillwalking was his thing. "Ah, when it's just you alone on a hill, it's marvelous, it's like..." He petered out with a headshake. Still, he was trying to express feelings he couldn't find words for, a good sign. I tried to encourage him further by telling him how, as a teenager on holiday with my family in Dubrovnik, I'd been wandering about by myself, when suddenly, around a headland, came a full-rigged three-masted sailing ship, white sails sweeping along in sunshine against a blue sky, and it made me feel totally desolate. Looking down into my drink, I said I couldn't then have brought myself to put into words why I felt like that. I stole a glance and saw he was staring at me, which boded well, though all he said was that hills often had Gaelic names. I learned that Ben More is a Big Mountain.

* * *

"...a party at Killearn."

That was the next step.

It got to be a regular thing, having drinks at Tennent's after swimming. I got his address out of him by saying I wanted to send him a Christmas card, though it was as if he couldn't see why I'd want to do such a thing, and I gave him my address in return and, yes, got a card back, signed, not very propitiously, "All the best."

It was time to move things forward.

My brother was giving a party in January at his house in Killearn. He was very friendly with a gay couple, God (short for Godfrey) and Drew. I wanted to see Fred's reaction when they danced together. They might even come up to us, assuming we were another couple; which might bring things to a head. I said, "You'd be welcome. The more the merrier." I tried to make it sound, not like a specific invitation to be my partner at the party, but more like my brother was keeping open house.

"Okay," he said, repeating the date as if it were a dentist's appointment.

I couldn't believe my luck when Dusty Springfield's "In Private" started playing, with its lyrics about a secret, and God and Drew made an event of dancing together, their moves close and coordinated. Fred was watching them.

"They're gay," I said. No reply.

I said it louder and added, "Totally out," wondering if he'd know what that meant.

The face he turned to me was blank before he came up with, "They're very bold." Was he communicating awareness of gay culture? "Isn't he bold?" was one of the camp lines between Julian and Sandy in an old radio program of which I had cassettes. But there was no knowingness in how Fred said it.

"Bold? Not these days. People are getting pretty accepting." He said nothing, and I added, "If girls can dance together, why not guys?"

He seemed to go rigid—from fear?—from determination?—from both? I wondered if he thought I was asking him to dance. I didn't want to risk all by a premature move and drive the mouse back into its hole, so I just suggested we investigate the food.

I wasn't unhopeful that I'd made progress. He stuck by my side all evening. He made no attempt to ask any of the women to dance; though perhaps he just didn't dance at all. I kept positioning us close to God and Drew, hoping they'd come up to us; preferable, I thought, to taking him to meet them.

But after he'd driven me home, he said I wouldn't be seeing him at the pool for a while. I waited for an explanation, then found he wasn't going to give one, not even something vague about work commitments or *family things* or whatever. Given what I'd thought of as our growing closeness, this felt like a determined snub. Without a word, I got out and slammed the car door behind me.

* * *

"We saw Torch Song Trilogy."

He remembered that films got us there.

After the party there was no sign of him at the pool, neither on our Wednesdays nor on other nights I tried. I gave up on him. What was the point of pursuing someone so unresponsive? Even as just a friend, he'd be wearing. But after six weeks, I gave it one more shot and phoned him, speaking as if there'd been no rift and only a few days had passed since we were last in touch. I decided on the "What about that drink?" tactic, which had worked before, though a riskier version because we'd never spoken of going to the cinema. "What about that film?"

"Okay." Even his unwelcome-obligation voice had nostalgic charm. When we took our seats, his thigh was against mine, but I got no message that that was anything other than what happened when a guy was tall.

I kept a lookout, especially in the programs of revival cinemas and film clubs, for films with unclothed male bodies in them or a gay element, but which also presented plausible other reasons for seeing them: *A Room with a View* (literature!), *My Beautiful Laundrette* (racism, Thatcherism, etc.), *Cabaret*. *Maurice* would have been too in-your-face, but I risked *Torch Song Trilogy* ("I loved Anne Bancroft in *The Graduate*").

He was silent driving me home, and when he came in for a post-film drink, a habit I'd got him into, he said in a voice of genuine puzzlement, "Why do people want to dress up in women's clothes?" Nothing against being gay as such, I noticed.

"Well," I said with an appallingly jaunty grin, "a lot of those who do are women."

The joke passed him by. As I disappeared into the kitchen for glasses, I added, as though it were a subject I didn't have much familiarity with, "I suppose some gay men do it, but most don't. I mean, God and Drew at that party don't."

As he went to pour his third whisky he managed to miss the glass and pour it onto his armchair. After I'd worked on the spillage with a wet cloth, the chair wasn't fit for sitting in and he moved across to the settee where I was sitting.

I asked, "Does AIDS worry you?" That could easily be given a heterosexual context if the conversation didn't go in the right direction, and then, suddenly, the game was played out. I didn't care any longer whether these maneuvers worked or whether they didn't, and before he could reply I leaned across and kissed him on the lips. His response was a child's puckered kiss on the cheek. What had sometimes seemed his permanent look of puzzlement vanished. He smiled joyously and said, "The ship coming round the headland."

Today I find it so lovable, that reference to the beautiful ship bearing the life I'd felt shut out from, but I didn't find it lovable at the time. The tedious trudge of getting him to this point promised an equally tedious future, despite the fact that he was talking eagerly about "this relationship." After sleeping with him two or three times, during which he was like a patient chattering about a medical procedure, I told him that I didn't think we had a future, not really.

He showed no surprise or disappointment. He just nodded and said, "I'll take some whisky," making it sound like paracetamol for a headache.

* * *

So I drove him down the road of self-harm. Because of me, he got drunk again and again, and now, thirty-odd years later, he was dying, lonely in a care home that he was liable to be turfed out of because his brother might not continue helping with the fees—I seemed to remember something about his brother being anti-gay, which could explain a lot. I drove Fred into something else as well, as I discovered later.

It was a fortnight before I mentioned to Alex the infidelity of receiving a letter from Fred, but I wasn't going to make a secret of visiting Fred, maybe helping with the fees, too. Alex was at his computer, working on his book about World War I, when I interrupted to tell him about the letter. Somehow, handing it to him to read would have been another betrayal of Fred. I was already guilty, since receiving the letter, of letting Fred down again, though I didn't know that then. I explained to Alex how I'd set Fred on the downward path by dumping him after leading him to fall in love with me.

"Isn't that a bit self-important? It sounds like he was already well on the way to alcoholism when you met him, so not your fault." Alex's tone of voice made it clear that settled the matter. He resumed typing.

"Ah, but when I met him, he was in the closet, anxious, no idea how to live the life he dreamed of. Yes, a person in that situation might need a drink to get him through, but it would have stopped if I'd not let him down."

He paused his typing. "Did you ever learn why he cut off contact with you without explanation?"

"Is it so incomprehensible that you draw back for a bit when you're scared and cautious and anxious, trembling on the brink of a huge step which could also mean a breach with your brother?"

"Or he cuts off contact in order to get rid of you because you're being a pest. And when it doesn't work and you still phone him, he decides on a different strategy: give the pest a charity fuck or two and hope that does the trick. So it's thigh against thigh in the cinema, upsetting his whisky so he can move across and snuggle up on the settee with you." The matter was settled again.

"*It wasn't like that!*" I shouted it. "You couldn't say something like that if you'd seen the look on his face, in his eyes, the night we…. It was real, he was following his feelings at last."

His smile was so wise you'd think he wasn't disconcerted at all. "Look, Gavrilo Princip did *not* cause the First World War."

"Who?"

"The man who assassinated the Archduke Ferdinand. Picking him out to blame for the war means ignoring everything else leading up to it, arms races and alliances and nationalism and imperialism and government crises and economics." The matter was settled again.

And, yes, for about a month, it was settled. I even wondered if Fred picked up the wrong bag in the changing room deliberately. I told myself I would visit Fred sometime, but given all the things that had happened to him in the thirty years before I met him and the thirty-plus years since, it was obviously over the top to blame myself for his plight. And then, after a month, this conviction came away like a filling from a tooth, and I knew that there can be pivotal episodes that turn a life irrevocably, like that Thomas Hardy heroine sending a valentine to a staid old farmer and setting tragedy in motion. I couldn't evade responsibility: Fred being led on by me and then dumped had been such an episode.

Alex was out when I dialed the number of Crichton Lodge.

"My name is Jamie Semple. I'm an old friend of one of your residents, Fred Archibald. He wrote saying he'd like me to visit."

"I'm sorry to have to break the news, but Alfred has passed away, about a month ago."

She said, "Are you still there, Mr. Semple?" But she seemed a bit distracted and added, "Excuse me a moment."

After a while the phone was picked up again. "I thought I recognized the name. Alfred said he was expecting to hear from you, but if he passed away first, he made us write down a message for you." She switched to a reading voice. "I'm sorry I wasted your time. I always mess up. They were good times."

"What was he getting at?"

"I'm afraid I couldn't say. He said we were to tell you just that, what I read out. His wife may know more—his ex-wife, I should say, but she was here several times before he passed away."

She said, "Are you still there, Mr. Semple?"

"Thank you very much, but I'll leave it there. It could be upsetting for his wife, his ex-wife, to bother her about what Fred meant, reminding her of... Some things are best left to rest." I heard myself manage to sound almost hearty.

* * *

This story first appeared in the After Dinner Conversation—February 2023 issue.

Discussion Questions

1. Alex argues, "Gavrilo Princip did *not* cause the First World War." What does this mean, and do you think it applies to Jamie's relationship with Fred?
2. Even though Fred wasn't very emotive or talkative, what do you think the real story of Fred and Jamie's relationship was from Fred's perspective?
3. To what extent do you think Jamie encouraged Fred to have homosexual experiences and feelings, and to what extent do you think Fred already has had those feelings and was waiting for the opportunity to act on them?
4. Do you think Jamie owed Fred anything for, potentially, setting him down a road of drinking?
5. What do think the conversation would have been, if Jamie had made it to talk to Fred before he died?

* * *

The Stone Piles

Jesse Rowell

* * *

Sitting over a plate of scrambled eggs with his orange hunting vest hugging his shoulders, the boy's father told stories of the hunt. He showed how he sighted a deer in his rifle's scope and pulled the trigger. The smell of sweat and leaves filled the kitchen as the father talked, and the child listened. The boy imagined his father chasing the animal, following its blood trail across the scattered leaves until cornering it somewhere in the forest. Then blam! A final shot to the head like he had been practicing with rubber bands on his stuffed animals.

"Maybe someday, Gregory," his mom said. "Someday, your dad will take you hunting?"

The boy's father looked off in the distance and shrugged each time the suggestion came up, and the boy watched him. Gregory dreamed of the day his father would shout hurrah, wallop him on the back, and point at the animal they had shot together. He held himself still listening for his response. But his father never committed to a hunting lesson. Instead, the man only heaved himself out of his chair for a shower and a nap.

"Come on, honey," she coaxed his father one autumn day. She held his forearm affectionately against the table. "Isn't it time you take him out? You can have him practice shooting something small by the stone piles. You don't have to take him up into the mountains."

Gregory's father pressed his lips together, inhaled through his nose, and looked down at his son. The child straightened his shoulders and looked for lines of approval on his father's face.

"Yeah, small things first. Target practice by the stone piles."

The stone piles. The place sounded magical to the child, a place where dragons and wizards tangled. He spent afternoons daydreaming about them, cultivating trees and gardens in his mind, building a fort behind slabs of stone. He would hunt porcupines with a stick sword replaced by a real gun. Not the harmless kind of porcupines, but the kind of monsters that ran wild in his imagination, shooting quills and blinding heroes.

Weeks passed, and the boy thought his father had forgotten his promise. He watched his face at dinner, and when he left the table, he looked up at his mom.

"I'll remind him, sweetie," she assured him.

Gregory never heard his mom remind him about shooting practice or the stone piles, but he thought she might ask him while they lay in bed, in the whisk of whispered words they shared sometimes.

The stone piles should have caves to explore and a chest filled with treasure. Gregory planned to set boobytraps to protect his secrets, nets with rocks hanging above entrances that could be loosened at any moment to crash upon an enemy's head. His classmates would ask to be a part of the stone piles tribe, and they would adopt some of the stray cats that crouched in the fields, and they would all play deep into the long afternoons.

On the bus ride home from school, he stared out the window and dreamed of his fort by the stone piles. Pastures passed, and sometimes roadkill, which the older boys claimed got cooked in cafeteria lunches. It made Gregory glad to have his lunchbox each time he glimpsed a deer crumpled on the side of the road. His sturdy lunchbox, its metal surface depicting a space battle from a movie he had never seen, with its heroes shooting laser cannons at spaceships. The stone fort should have laser cannons. He traced his fingers over the raised images on his lunchbox.

A bully flicked his ear. "Hey, Petee. Your family too poor to buy hot lunch?"

Gregory shrugged and tightened his lips. The cafeteria lunches looked tasty enough, hot pizza and burritos, but what if there was roadkill in them? He didn't want to admit to the bully that his soggy honey sandwich sat uneaten in his lunchbox.

"That space movie is dumb," the bully taunted.

The bus creaked to a stop, and its doors hissed open. Gregory jumped down the stairs and tumbled to the ground, his lunchbox spilling its contents across the gravel road. The sandwich in its wax paper, a granola bar, and juice box, all on display for the bemused faces pressed against the bus windows as it drove off in a cloud of dust.

He wiped grit off his teeth with the back of his hand and waited for the bus to disappear. The wind came down from the mountains blowing dust and rustling the leaves in the culvert. He bent down to clean off the pieces of his lunch in the way he imagined his father did with animals left on the ground.

The juice box had tumbled under the metal bars of the road's cattle guard, a barrier meant to stop cattle no longer living here. He dismissed the idea of retrieving his juice box. His arm might get caught between the bars, the horror of being trapped against the ground and yelling for help in hopes that his mom would hear him.

Walking home, he began to imagine his stone fort again, its smooth and rounded edges, when a bundle of black fur interrupted his thoughts. A stray kitten, no more than a few months old, hobbled away from Gregory in halting hops toward an abandoned trailer. It turned to watch him from under a doorstep, its green eyes staring at him from the shadows.

He felt revulsion as he watched the kitten back itself under the wreck, a feeble pathetic thing unaware that he posed no danger. It cowered as it watched him, ready to recede deeper into the shadows if he got closer. He felt angry, but he didn't know why. The thing's suffering made him want to hurt it more, to drive the animal out of his thoughts so he could return to daydreaming. Seeing it here made the desolation uglier, an ugliness that told him he would never win his father's approval, that he would never go hunting, that he would never find the stone piles.

Its mom must have abandoned it, he thought. She wasn't here to hiss at him and carry her child away by the nape of its neck, lick the goop crusting its eyes. Not worth the effort to teach it how to hunt. She had left it to starve in the dust, spent of energy, unaware and dumb.

Gregory placed his honey sandwich on top of wax paper, crunching like dry leaves as he laid it on the ground. The kitten did not move toward the sandwich. It did not acknowledge that food had been placed in its proximity. Gregory waited for it to move, waited for it to show a sign of gratitude. It felt like a staring contest. Gregory kicked the sandwich like a kickball at recess.

When he opened his eyes, eyes that had clenched shut when he had kicked the sandwich, he saw pieces of soggy bread splattered against the hill, a mash of dull beige indistinguishable from the browning leaves and dirt. The hollow under the doorstep was empty. No green eyes peered out to watch him. Angry that it had run away, angry that he had started to feel sympathy for its gross life, he ran up the road until he reached the fence surrounding his home.

That night over spaghetti dinner, he thought about the kitten as he watched over his fork while his father slurped up tangled braids of red noodles. Gregory thought about what food he could hide in his lunchbox to feed it after school, something his parents wouldn't notice missing from the pantry. Maybe late at night, he could steal some sugar and put it in a bag for the kitten. White sugar made his jaw tingle when he sneaked handfuls of it into his mouth while they were sleeping.

"Watcha got on your mind, son? You look like you're planning something that will get you in trouble."

Gregory opened his mouth to answer, but his mom placed a hand on his arm. "He ate all his lunch at school today. No wasted food. We're proud of him for that."

"Humph." His father shrugged. "It's not that hard to learn how to eat. Basic skill for survival. An animal who doesn't know how to eat is diseased. I came across an elk drooling like a fool just staring at me. Didn't move an inch when I approached. I didn't shoot it. No sport in killing a diseased animal. You know, you should pack his lunch with some of that flank venison. Bet he would be the only kid in school eating meat that his dad shot."

She looked pensively down at Gregory. "Okay, maybe a little. It might be hard for him to chew. And, you know, the lead fragments."

"It's not that hard to learn how to eat."

The venison stunk up his lunchbox the next day at school so that everything tasted like deer meat. He tried sneaking out pieces of honey sandwich, a metallic thwomp each time he closed the lid of his lunchbox, but the smell drifted across the cafeteria table. Kids wrinkled their noses.

"What the fuck are you eating, Petee? A shit sandwich? Petee eats shit."

He closed his lunchbox and stuffed it deep inside his backpack. When he returned to class, his teacher shook her head and instructed him to leave his backpack outside the classroom door. Classmates snickered at him that afternoon on the bus ride home.

At the cattle guard, he dropped the remains of the honey sandwich between the metal grates. He walked to the trailer where he had last seen the kitten and held out the deer meat. No kitten sat beneath the steps. He placed the meat on wax paper and backed away. When he reached the hill above the trailer park, he thought he saw something dark, maybe the kitten, pulling the deer meat back under the trailer.

The days grew shorter as hunting season dragged toward its close. Gregory's father talked about shooting a deer in the neck when dusk had nearly stolen his light, how he had seen the animal far off in the distance, and how he had crept up the hill until he was sure his bullet would connect, but stumbled on a rock and missed its torso. He recalled a time when he was younger and more athletic, how he could kill a deer with a single arrow from his compound bow, certain it caused the animal no pain.

Gregory didn't understand all the words his father used but pictured him pushing through the oak brush to stalk the animal. He looked back at his mom, hope tempered with frustration.

"This weekend?" she asked. "You can take him to one of the empty lots and have him practice."

"Sure," his father said in a way that the child knew he was lying, the higher pitch to his voice, but Gregory grinned in happy confusion after being rousted out of bed early the following day by rough hands and coffee breath. "Come on, son. Let's go hunting."

They walked past trailers and fallen fencing. Gregory could barely contain his excitement as their feet crunched against the gravel. He knew the stone piles lay somewhere beyond the trailer park, somewhere he had never seen.

"The lesson starts before we get there," his father said as they walked. "Never point a gun at me, you got that? Even if your finger is nowhere near the trigger. You got that?"

Gregory nodded solemnly.

"This is a .22, so you won't get much kickback. We'll have you start on something small, like rabbits. The fastest way to find a rabbit's nest is by its smell. It's going to stink, a really nasty sweet smell, you know? Like when you used to pee your bed and tried hiding it from us for a couple days."

Gregory's cheeks flushed with shame, but he looked up at his father and straightened his shoulders, determined that he would win his father's approval today out of all days, that he would shoot an animal dead in the head, and his father would shout hurrah and wallop him on the back. His father would be proud of him, give him that same soft look of adoration that his mom sometimes gave him, and help him build a great fort at the stone piles.

They walked past a trailer's tangled fencing that had fallen into deep disrepair, the first of the trailers that had been vacated when the park was condemned. Insulation leaked out against the broken edges of wood paneling and glass. Smudges of rust ran down its side. Building materials for our fort, Gregory thought. They could build a tower like the ones on castles where they would hunt for deer high up in the air.

Gregory's father lifted him over a section of lattice fencing, a lovely white fence that had once surrounded somebody's home or maybe a garden. It felt good to be lifted up, strong hands gripping him under the armpits and setting him down on the other side, a father's strength that could easily rocket him up into the sky and catch him when he returned, or crush him into the ground on a whim. His father stopped before stepping over. "What's that there?" He bent down to look at the fence.

Nestled between the slats was the head of the black kitten. A trail of red ants moved across the fence to swarm its face. Yellow snot pooled beneath its chin as ants picked at the mucus covering its nose. Gregory thought he could hear the ants, a strange rustling sound that did not stop.

"Dead cat," his father said. He pushed at the fence with the side of his boot but jumped back when the kitten meowed.

It lifted its head and tried looking up at them through pus-filled eyes. Its head sunk down, and the ants kept picking at its face.

"Damn." He shook his head. "Parasites are eating it alive."

Gregory felt the same revulsion and anger rising inside him like the first day he saw the kitten cowering under a trailer. All the food he had laid out for it, the water bowl, and the blanket: all wasted efforts against the inevitable. Coaxing it out of its hole had prolonged the torture of its small, pathetic life. Where was its mom? She watched from a distance, snatching up the morsels of food instead of protecting her child. A betrayal.

His father placed the rifle in Gregory's hands. He felt the warmth at its base where his father had held it, and he felt the barrel's cold metal in his other hand.

"Well," he started. "Your mommy wanted you to practice on something small. Take a couple steps back and point at its head. I'll release the safety when you get the target lined up."

It took a moment for Gregory to realize what his father had asked him to do. He felt his blood drain from his face, his cheeks no longer red as he opened his mouth, but he could not speak. Instead, he looked from the rifle to the kitten, its fur slowly rising and falling as it struggled to breathe. The sound of ants came and went like wind against trees.

"Don't worry." He gestured toward the mountains. "I see this kind of thing in the wild all the time. They do this to their young, hobble them to kill them when their genetics are all wrong."

Gregory searched the hills for its mom, green eyes that had watched him drop leftover lunches on the ground. Why didn't she rush down here to save her child, hiss at them, and carry it away? He thought he could see her watching from the shadows, waiting for them to leave.

"That's a safe distance. Now aim for its head." His father nudged the barrel up.

Gregory looked down the top of the rifle at the kitten. The safety clicked off. He smelled the oil his father used to polish his guns, a smell he recognized from his father's hands. His father's hands held his shoulder and elbow to line up the rifle.

"Take a deep breath," he instructed. "Pull the trigger as you breathe out."

Gregory inhaled through his nose, held his breath, and hoped to hold it forever. He heard the sound of ants scurrying, scratching, scraping. Horrible sounds followed by another, a crack ripping through the air.

When he opened his eyes, eyes that had been clenched shut when he had pulled the trigger, he saw the kitten twisted on its side, the black mass of fur stretching for something it would never be able to reach.

"Goddammit!" his father cursed as he pulled the gun from Gregory's hands. "You don't let a thing suffer like that. Do you understand?"

He had wanted to miss. There would be no hiding this from his father.

"You don't look away from suffering. You deal with it." His father brought the gun down on the kitten's head.

Gregory looked away. The hills cast long shadows across the gray with the arrival of morning. The stone piles seemed impossibly far away now, somewhere beyond the leaves and ruins with nothing to hold on to.

* * *

This story first appeared in the After Dinner Conversation—November 2022 issue.

Discussion Questions

1. Gregory wants his father's approval, yet doesn't have the temperament for hunting. In the long term, how do you think Gregory will resolve these two conflicting issues as he grows up?

2. Gregory's father seems unable to show his approval of Gregory in ways suited to Gregory's interests. What would have to happen for Gregory's father to change and interact with Gregory as he is?

3. Gregory's father is traditional in his gender roles and interests. Can a traditional father still be a good father? Is Gregory's father a good father? Does it matter that Gregory's father seemed to understand Gregory was not suited for hunting and likely would not have taken him hunting, but for his mother's insistence?

4. Gregory "felt revulsion as he watched the kitten back itself under the wreck, a feeble pathetic thing unaware that he posed no danger." Why do you think Gregory was revulsed by a pathetic thing for failing to understand he posed no danger?

5. How should Gregory's father have dealt with the sick and dying kitten? Gregory's father says, "You don't look away from suffering. You deal with it." Is this true? Is this a lesson Gregory needed to learn?

* * *

The Only Punishment

Ville V. Kokko

* * *

The floor of the room was white, but three of the walls and the ceiling were light blue. His own bland pajamas were light green.

It was probably supposed to be calming, but it only angered Rats. He knew what this was—a fregging brainwashing facility, that's what. It didn't matter how *nice* they were trying to be. It was just a part of it.

He glanced angrily at the glass wall. It was the only window in the room, made of thick and unbreakable glass, and it showed nothing but a garden, so overgrown it looked more like a forest. Of course, this was supposed to be a *nice* view. Pretty trees and flowers and a pretty little fregging stream. It was so fregging blatant that he wondered how stupid the Authorities could be. Admittedly, he'd spent a lot of time staring at it while he was in his cell, but that was only because there was nothing else to do. The room was almost bare, with a bunk and a table and a side door to a small bathroom—and the big, unmovable door that led outside.

Of course, even Rats himself admitted it was in some ways better than where he used to live. But he'd still choose his old hole any day. It may have been stinky and loud and no bigger than this cell—but it was his. And he knew he wasn't going to walk out brainwashed to be a nice little fregging sheep when he went there.

Of course, Rats knew he could have been a better person. Nobody was perfect, and especially not in the slums. You couldn't afford it. But he *was* a good person, he knew that, as much as he could be. He stood up for his mates and helped people in need when he could afford to. He kept his word and his honor.

At one point, he'd even told it to them, when a couple of them were escorting him to one of their stupid, ineffective brainwashing sessions. He tried his best, he'd told them. The "crimes" they'd arrested him for, they had no idea what was really happening. Sure, he'd been violent, probably even killed someone—so what? They'd attacked first, and not just once. Of course, if you just came swooping to the scene in your fregging flying car at that moment, it would look like he was attacking, but it really wasn't like that. And if these guys were allowed to punish you for wrongdoing, why couldn't the people on the streets bust some heads too? Rats would never have hurt someone who didn't deserve it. And he lived down there, in the slums in the ruins—he knew what was going on and he had the right. *These* guys just came from somewhere outside and started kidnapping and brainwashing people.

Rats had seen what the victims became like, and they were too bad even for pity—he despised them. Like that tweet who ran the Charity Church. Of course, Rats had nothing against helping people, but he was such a fregging eunuch. Besides, he helped everyone equally, the zips and tooks as well as decent White people. Rats could even have understood staying outside the gangs and helping everyone regardless, but feeding the pests was only going to end up bad for everyone. Every time you helped a zip, you might as well be kicking a real person in the face.

But no, these high-and-mighty Authorities thought they knew everything better and made you love everyone equally. They'd never been ganged up on by the tooks or listen to yet another sobbing woman having been raped by the zips. They were "tolerant," which meant they only thought it was a crime if White people did it.

And the worst crime of all—wasn't that just what *they* were doing? Brainwashing good people to be like them? Truth be told, Rats feared nothing as much as it working on him. So far, it was having no effect at all, but he sensed vaguely that there was going to be more. And everyone knew it worked on almost anyone.

Everyone also knew that if it didn't, they'd just kill you. He was hoping they'd kill him.

Rats stared morosely out of the window. There were colorful birds in the trees. That almost cheered him up.

* * *

Some guards opened the door to bring in food. He'd tried fighting his way past them once, but it had been no use. He didn't even remember what happened other than that he'd been out cold almost immediately and woken up later with his meal neatly laid out and getting cold. The food was good, he had to admit, but he still ate grudgingly and left some over.

He took a nap, knowing that soon after lunch, it would be brainwashing time again. Sure enough, he was awoken by the sound of the door opening again.

"Hello," Jeremy said and stepped inside, flanked by a couple of guards. They also said hello, and one of them picked up his plate. Jeremy sounded friendly enough, and the two guards sounded business-like, but of course Rats wasn't fooled.

Jeremy was Rats' personal brainwasher. He was tall and stout and wore a mustache he could have done without, though Rats wasn't about to give him any fregging fashion tips. He must have been specifically trained to be pleasant; Rats sometimes found it hard to hate him, even knowing what he did. He even seemed a little sorry that they were doing this to Rats, although he'd also expressed a firm opinion that Rats had done wrong.

"You come to take me in for brainwashing?" Rats said sarcastically. He sensed that, carefully though Jeremy hid his feelings, calling it that was one thing that got to him.

Jeremy looked down at him inscrutably. "Actually, yes. Today we do what you would call the brainwashing."

It was an instinctive reaction. Rage and despair exploded Rats from where he was sitting on the bed and out toward his tormentors. He might have torn out Jeremy's throat.

But of course, he got nowhere. One of the guards pulled out some fancy techno weapon and pointed and clicked him into unconsciousness.

* * *

When Rats woke up, he found that he was tethered to a wheelchair. He also found that he was drugged somehow, because the thought of raging in despair died as soon as it was born. His head was fuzzy and there was an odd sense of pleasure. So, he had to contend himself with a quiet, nagging sense of despair.

"Aw, hell," he muttered, leaning his head back on a pillow. "I'm sorry about this."

Rats turned his head to the side and saw Jeremy, walking by him. And he saw that they were just about to walk past a door—room 3B, where all the previous brainwashing sessions had taken place.

So this was really it. It was going to be something different—the part where they broke you.

Idly, he wondered what all the other sessions had been about. He'd thought it had been ridiculous. They'd put this cap with all the wires on his head, and he'd been so furious and terrified they'd had to drug him like this at first, but then they'd done almost nothing. They'd just given him... history lessons. Things he didn't care about and barely paid attention to, though the device had forcibly input it in his brain and he'd noticed bits of it had stuck.

It was about the history of the City, and how the Authorities had come to be there. A lot of stuff about how it had once been a great, wealthy city where life had been much better, but then there had been a civil war and a collapse... And then the Authorities had come and they just had to do *something*. So they started a police force, and they started applying the dreaded Punishment. They didn't want to, but, the brain-movies said, they couldn't leave things as they were...

There had been more to it—whole three sessions of history—but this seemed to have been the point. And, as the drug's effect began to weaken, Rats realized something about this was starting to terrify him. Something that his brain had been working out on his own, while he wasn't looking, from all the stuff shoved into it. He could feel the dull terror before he was able to articulate the thought in his mind.

They really believed in it. They really believed they had to do this. They really wanted to help. That was why they were so fregging apologetic all the time; they even knew what they were doing was bad, but they thought they had to do it.

Thinking all this only took a few seconds. "It doesn't matter, you know," Rats heard himself saying.

"Pardon?"

Rats waved a hand, though it was a very small wave since his wrist was restrained. "Doesn't matter what you're all doing this for, Jeremy. It's still fregging brainwashing. It's just wrong. You can't do that to me, period. Doesn't matter what your reasons."

Jeremy sighed. "I know what you mean. But you're also wrong—it's not at all as bad as you think. And you do have a choice, in the end. And no, we won't kill you if you don't do as we want."

"Like freg you won't."

"Of course, I also know all of these are things real brainwashers would tell you beforehand. All I can say is, wait and see."

"Wait until I'm brainwashed and see?"

"I know, I know..."

"Because I can't make a choice after that, can I? You've... already made it for me."

"I know. It's not really... but there's no point in talking about this. And even though it's not like you imagine, we still think it might be a bad thing, because it's still too much like brainwashing. But we've also seen the alternative. And really, in some ways it's a lot like if you were simply educated the right way when you were little..."

Rats laughed hollowly. His head was starting to clear, although there was liable to be a migraine. Still, he didn't feel like fighting now.

"I hope I'll die. I'd rather. And in a sense, maybe I will, anyway, if there's nothing left but your zombie slave."

Jeremy didn't reply. Instead, he opened a door: Room A1. "We're here."

* * *

Rats was past despair and fear. He didn't struggle. This was going to be the end for him anyway; all he wanted to do now was to guilt Jeremy, to somehow show him that he was wrong and Rats was right. To somehow show this nice man that he was killing him.

The thought that Jeremy was killing him out of kindness was almost scarier than the same thought about the Authorities, because Jeremy had a face, was a man. Rats found himself for the first time less afraid of what would happen to him and more spiritually terrified at the state of humankind. Atrocities done for good intentions, how did you cope with that? They were walking around doing evil things and they thought they were good. He'd met hypocrites and idiots before, of course, but this was all so... so *philosophical*.

As in Room 3B, there was a chair with restraints in front of a monitor, with ominous technothingies hanging over it and on its sides. Rats let himself be attached without opposition, with only a shiver.

The complicated plastic harness on his head was even more complicated this time. It took minutes for Jeremy and some others to put it on. Finally, they told him to relax. A big text saying "TESTING" solidified slowly into his view. It wasn't on the monitor but seemingly hovering in the air and moving with his eyes. This, too, was familiar.

"Need some adjustments at 36 and 42," someone said out of sight. Someone fiddled with the probes atop his skull. TESTING came up again, looking just the same in his opinion, but this time they deemed everything to be working all right.

At least the clamps on his head were comfortable. He could even move his neck a little and lean on a kind of pillow. It would still get uncomfortable, he knew this from experience, but only after several minutes.

Then he began to see auras and his head swam. He could feel his hair standing up from the electricity. It was beginning.

* * *

Rats blacked out very briefly, and when he came back to, his mind was floating in a fuzzy imaginary space that mostly concealed the reality around him. He remembered where he was but couldn't really see or feel or hear it. Nor smell. Instead, a familiar smell rose up; something mildly unpleasant but familiar, a smell whose origin he didn't know and that he had barely noticed before. A smell from his home streets.

It felt almost as if he was there again. They were raising up his memories, or feeding him a new version of them—who knew. He had a vague sense at first of just being there, superficially skipping through all kinds of familiar scenarios. Then the show began.

He saw himself doing things—and soon he realized these

were the crimes he was being accused of—and not too long after that, he began laughing in the real world, hollow, a little manic, a sound that pushed its way even into this induced dream. Because he had won; they weren't going to brainwash him after all.

He saw himself mugging someone; in a gang fight; pushing around some zip kids; stealing from a shop. He even saw the one that had got him arrested and that had secretly been troubling him—a violent scuffle where he'd stabbed more than one person, starting from another gang dispute.

But he also saw that he had been right, all along. He'd had no choice; or, it hadn't been that bad, after all; or, they totally had it coming; or, he was just standing up for his buddies. Usually it was about all of these each time. He remembered now why he'd done those things, and he didn't regret them at all. Even the last big fight—they'd had it coming, and he was only standing up for himself, and they would have done worse.

These fregging idiots had thought they could make him cower in front of them by showing how bad he was—but in the cold light of the facts, he didn't regret anything.

The images died out, and the real world began to swim back into focus. Rats struggled to gain control of his mouth to say something. But instead, he heard Jeremy's voice next to his ear.

"That was the first part—how it felt like to you."

Then the virtual reality snapped back on, and Rats was seeing something different.

He was an awkward, fat man, walking in the street, looking around nervously, sweating uncomfortably. He'd only come to this part of town because he was running out of money and there was a job, but he was scared...

He was a member of a gang, and it was so familiar he thought it was his own, until he realized it was the other one...

He was a kid, walking around and joking with some other kids—they forgot to be afraid because they were zips for a while...

He was a shopkeeper, struggling to make ends meet, constantly afraid of thieves because they were everywhere, but really, if they only stole from him, he would be lucky they hadn't hurt him...

And then *he was scared to death when this big thug stepped in front of him. And he took all his money and he would go hungry that week, but that wasn't enough, the leering thug pushed him around and almost made him wet his pants, and he went away fighting tears of rage.*

...The gangs got into a fight, and the one he was in now was clearly in the right, but those other bastards went pushing way past their rights and hurt some of his mates. And one of them was Rats.

...A couple of big, mean white bullies started shouting at them, and they called them names and said a lot of nasty things they didn't even understand properly, and they were afraid they would die if they didn't play nice, and the bullies hit them and pushed them to the ground and it hurt.

...He was counting out his money and it was not enough, it was never enough, and he cursed the fregging thieves who seemed to have taken as much stuff as he had managed to sell.

He was in the other gang again, and they got into mouthing off with the enemy, and those bastards went way too far, and when the fight began, one of them pulled out a knife, totally out of nowhere, and he was stabbed, and the pain was horrible, and he fell down to the ground and knew he was going to die...

* * *

Rats actually blacked out again when he died in his dream. When he snapped back into reality, he screamed hoarsely.

This hadn't been just images or information, it had been emotions, it had been perspectives, it had been *being* the other person. Yet, he wasn't. He was Rats. And he was a monster, a leering, terrifying bully, a vicious thug from the other gang, a faceless, heartless thief, the face of death and pain at the other end of the dagger. You saw other people that way all the time, but never yourself. You *couldn't* see yourself like that. All the defense mechanisms had been stripped away, all that the ego normally relied on, and the contempt, hatred, fear and above all pain of others struck at him like knives to the soul.

He was twisting and struggling in his chair—he realized as he came back to reality—and shouting something. It might have been *"Kill me!"*

If he had felt such things toward someone else, he *would* have killed them.

A needle injected another dose of calming drug into his arm. He twitched a few last times and then just stayed there, panting. He was physically calmed down, but the drug didn't really make the pain go away. He still felt numbly horrible.

"I'm sorry, Rats," Jeremy said by his ear. "It will get better. That was the second part: how it felt to the others. Now comes the third part—the multiplex view."

The virtual reality engulfed him again.

* * *

Rats calmed down, as if by command, which it obviously was. He now had a sense of surveying the whole city as if floating above it, and also along the streets. And then he started seeing the same events again, from a point of view he couldn't have imagined. It was as if he were everyone and no one; several people at once but beyond any of them. And both taking part and an outsider.

There were both of the gangs, both really about the same, but both hating each other's guts because of old events—events, he saw, that had a lot to do with everyone looking out for their own group and being unfair toward the other. Any time either gang took revenge, the other thought they'd gone too far; and then they'd take revenge again, and the others would think they were starting it all over again when the score had just been settled.

There was the mugged fat man, but there was also the mugger, himself. The mugger thought he needed the money more badly and it served the guy right for coming to the wrong part of town, but he wouldn't have thought so if he knew how the fat man felt and how *he* needed the money. And even if he had really needed the money more, he shouldn't have gone on a power trip and frightened the guy so much. But the fat man was also wrong, because he feared and hated the mugger and saw him as only a monster who was doing it almost for fun. It had been wrong to rob him, Rats realized, but he also saw why he hadn't seen this before. He had been stupid and selfish, and he had been bad, but he had never meant to be *that* bad.

There were the zip kids, who'd done nothing bad and just wanted to goof around with their friends and barely even understood about this whole race thing, except they were already starting to learn they needed to be afraid, and ashamed of who they were, and that wasn't right. And there was Rats and the other guy who had pushed them around, and *they* had been taught to despise and hate zips, and even when they looked at a couple of kids, they didn't even see them as real kids. They were very wrong, but they didn't see it; again, they were not really monsters, just stupid and blind to the unfairness of their own thinking. They would have never knowingly been so unfair. In a blinding flash of double feeling, Rats was himself pushing the kid down and the kid at the same time, and he understood himself as he had never before. He was hurting a kid of less than ten years old, but all he saw at the moment was... this annoying object that he hated and wanted to be rid of somehow. He'd balked after that, seeing he was going too far, but it was nothing compared to the kid's terror and emotional hurt, worse than the physical pain.

And there was the merchant struggling for money and counting every penny and feeling hurt and exposed when he was stolen from, but there was also the thief who was also struggling for money. At that point, Rats felt less guilty about stealing than about stupidly thinking he wasn't hurting anyone. At the very least, even though he had a real need, he should have taken less. Probably not even that.

Finally, there was the fight where he may have killed people. And he saw a couple of gangs, mirror images of each other, trading insults, escalating it because they were itching to fight. What struck him was that they had really thought that pent-up anger and defending your honor against mere words had been worth it, had justified it—this fight where people had been hurt and even, perhaps, killed.

Rats' mind was flooded with new thoughts, feelings, understandings. He could barely think straight, but he knew he had a lot to think about. Had he known of it, he would have been grateful of being made to drift into peaceful, normal sleep afterwards.

* * *

Rats awoke feeling strangely light and empty. He wasn't sure, but he may actually have been feeling good. He sensed through his eyelids that morning light was flooding through the window in his cell.

"Good morning, Rats. How are you feeling now?"

Rats opened his eyes and saw Jeremy sitting on a chair by his bed in the cell. He was smiling, but looking at him with some concern. A surge of emotions flashed through Rats' mind, starting with the negative but settling down to something surprisingly positive. He realized how much he would have liked Jeremy if he hadn't had such strong reasons not to. The man had a quiet kind of strength, different from what he was used to on the streets but very real.

And as for those reasons...

"That... was that the brainwashing?"

"Yes. All of it," Jeremy said. "And now I can tell you something else too, that you couldn't have understood before."

"What's that?"

"I've been through that as well. Most of us here have."

"You used to be criminals?"

"Some of us, but that's not what I meant. We wanted to make sure we were doing the right thing in the end."

"I'm not sure what..."

"We made ourselves see this 'brainwashing' from the point of view of the subjects as well. I've seen what it feels like, both before and after, the way you felt how you had hurt people. Of course, we can't *prove* it's right that way, because we need to have the multiplex debriefing for our sanity, and we need to take an active hand in designing what it shows. But let me tell you, it was a real eye-opener. That's why we're so sorry we need to make you do something like this against your will."

"But I get to make a free choice what to do now? Is that what you've been getting at?"

"Yes. Everyone's free to go after this, because they've had their punishment and so few people go back to committing crimes as they used to. Of course, if they do, we may have to arrest them again and prescribe old-fashioned jail time or counselling. Fortunately, that really is rare."

"Yeah, that was punishment all right..."

"Personally, I think it's the one right punishment for anyone. Just to *see* the harm... although we can't leave it at that or it might break people for good. I... hope you feel you've recovered by now and understand more? And why we're doing this?"

"Yeah... I guess I do, though I have a lot of thinking to do. Before I decide anything, too."

"Of course. And a lot of people want to study after this, too."

"Study?"

"Psychology and sociology and evolutionary psychology and things like that. To put words to what they've been directly shown. You could never understand these things so well from just reading books... I mean, it's the kind of thing you can tell people and often they'll nod, yes, of course, I understand that, and then they go right back to thinking like they did before. But anyway, once you have understood them like this, the theory can help you put it all together."

"Books?"

"Also, videos and interactive computer programs, if you prefer. Also, novels and movies if you want to explore it through art."

"Yeah, I might... look at some of those."

"You can do as you wish. This was the last time you had to stay in this cell. You can move to the open ward now. There will also be others like you who you can talk to."

* * *

When Rats made his decision after several surprisingly pleasant days, he realized it had been at the back of his head from the start. He asked if he could go and help at the Charity Church. He could. And so he worked there, patiently, day to day, helping the helpless and enduring the threats and taunts of people like he used to be. He had to keep reminding himself of why they were that way, but he never did forget, and so he was always patient. He even got through to some of them and converted them to work with him. Little by very little, they made the City a better place to live for everyone.

He never did figure out whether it was really brainwashing or not.

* * *

This story first appeared in the After Dinner Conversation—February 2022 issue.

Discussion Questions

1. Do you think what they did to Rats was brainwashing? What is your working definition of brainwashing and how does it apply, or not apply, to what happened to Rats?
2. If this treatment really existed, do you think it would work? What percent of the time do you think it would work?
3. Is there really a difference between understanding how your actions affect others, and actually living the interactions from their perspective? What, if anything, is the difference, and why does it exist?
4. Traditional prisons hold your body, but you maintain your free will within its confines. Is forcing someone to live an experience without free will an acceptable form of punishment?
5. If a punishment like the one in the story were possible, would you support its implementation? What levels of crimes would it be acceptable for, and what level would be too low to warrant its use?

* * *

Author Information

The Man Who Killed the Dog

Robert Collings is a retired lawyer living and writing in Pitt Meadows, B.C. His publications include the short memoir, "The Spaghetti Party – A Memoir of My Father" and "The Man Who Threw the Punch." He has additionally published "Carl the Mover," "Boardwalk and the Upper Crust," "Boardwalk," "The Tears of the Gardener," "Thong Man" and "The Secret Agent." These and other short stories are contained in Robert's collection, *Life in the First Person*. He has also written a satirical novella, *One Dog's Life*.

The Free Will of Professor Sturmhauser

Rosalind Goldsmith lives in Toronto. She is a literacy tutor for adults and began writing short fiction seven years ago. Her stories have been published in journals in the USA, the UK, and Canada. She loves to write stories about people from all walks of life who are confronted with thorny ideas and/or impossible situations.

Taps

Paul Hilding practiced law in California for 35 years before retiring to Idaho where he has recently begun trying his hand at fiction writing. "Taps" is his first submission for publication. Paul is currently working on a novel loosely based on battles he fought with the insurance industry during his legal career. Hilding also serves on the nonprofit Advocates for the West, an environmental law firm based in Boise.

They Got Their Show

Garrett Davis is a plumber by day and writer whenever he can muster the courage. He lives in B.C.

Christmas In Ushuaia

Matias Travieso-Diaz is an engineer and attorney, born in Cuba and retired after half a century of professional practice. Following retirement, he has taken up creative writing and is the author of numerous stories of various lengths and genres. His stories have been published or accepted for publication by about forty paying literary magazines and journals.

All My Tomorrows

J. Grace Pennington has been telling stories since she could talk and writing them down since age five. Now she lives in the great state of Texas, where she writes as much as adult life permits. When she's not writing, she enjoys reading good books, having adventures with her husband, and looking up at the stars.

The Momentary Paradise

Olga Pavlinova Olenich is a widely published Australian writer whose work appears in local and international publications. Her prose and poems have been broadcast on national radio and have featured in national newspapers. Publications include collection *Best Australian Humorous Writing, The Best Travel Writing Volume 11* and *Best Australian Poems*.

The Causes Of The First World War

Paul Brownsey is a former member of the philosophy faculty at Glasgow University, Scotland, and likes attempting to embody philosophical issues within short fiction, here questions about the extent of our responsibility for evils suffered by others. His book, *His Steadfast Love and Other Stories*, was a Lambda Literary Awards finalist, and received a starred review from *Publishers Weekly*. Recent work has appeared in *Orca, Event, Ambit,* and *Two Thirds North*.

The Stone Piles

Jesse Rowell is a technology consultant and science fiction author based in Seattle. He has been featured in multiple publications, including NPR and several literary journals. He can be found at *www.jesserowell.com*

The Only Punishment

Ville V. Kokko is a PhD student in Philosophy and an aspiring writer of both fiction and nonfiction living in Turku, Finland. So far, he has had several short stories and articles published in both English and Finnish. Some of his favorite topics to read and write about are philosophy, speculative fiction, and combinations of the two.

Additional Information

Reviews

If you enjoyed reading these stories, please consider doing an online review. It's only a few seconds of your time, but it is very important in continuing the series. Good reviews mean higher rankings. Higher rankings mean more sales and a greater ability to release stories.

Print Books

https://www.afterdinnerconversation.com

Purchase our growing collection of print anthologies, "Best of," and themed print book collections. Available from our website, online bookstores, and by order from your local bookstore.

Podcast Discussions/Audiobooks

https://www.afterdinnerconversation.com/podcastlinks

Listen to our podcast discussions and audiobooks of After Dinner Conversation short stories on Apple, Spotify, or wherever podcasts are played. Or, if you prefer, watch the podcasts on our YouTube channel or download the .mp3 file directly from our website.

Patreon

https://www.patreon.com/afterdinnerconversation

Get early access to short stories and ad-free podcasts. New supporters also get a free digital copy of the anthology *After Dinner Conversation– Season One*. Support us on Patreon!

Book Clubs/Classrooms

https://www.afterdinnerconversation.com/book-club-downloads

After Dinner Conversation supports book clubs! Receive free short stories for your book club to read and discuss!

Social

Connect with us on Facebook, YouTube, Instagram, TikTok, Substack, and Twitter.